The Lost Treasures of Padre Mine

A novelization by David Noble

Lulu Press

David Noble

The Lost Treasures of Padre Mine: t

ISBN 979-8-9910855-1-9

Manufactured by Lulu Press, Inc.

700 Park Offices Drive Suite 250 Research Triangle, NC 27709

www.lulu.com

For information about permission to reproduce selections from this book, contact Noble Park Films at info@nobleparkfilms.com

~Prologue ~
A Brief History of Padre Mine
by Paul Harden
Secretary, Socorro County Historical Society

https://socorro-history.org

In 1797, a dying Spanish soldier told his priest, Father LaRue, of gold in the mountains north of El Paso del Norte, today's El Paso. When the soldier died, Father LaRue organized a small expedition to find the gold.

Following the soldier's instructions, they traveled north from El Paso until three small peaks could be seen. From there, they crossed the Jornada del Muerto to the San Andreas mountains. After days of exploration, they found a spring at the base of the solitary peak, just as the old soldier had said. On the far side of the peak, a rich vein of gold in a deep canyon, southwest of the springs, was located.

LaRue, a Jesuit priest, summoned monks and Indians from the monastery at Chihuahua to help mining the gold. So plentiful was the yellow ore, they built a smelter to shape the gold into ingots and crude coins. They were stacked along the wall of the mine tunnel, accumulating an impressive cache.

After many weeks working the mines, the men were running low on food and supplies. Padre LaRue and some of his monks traveled to Mesilla to stock up on supplies. As they bought items purchasing their goods with their gold coins, it raised a red flag. Spanish law prohibited the Jesuits from owning gold or a mine. Padre LaRue was found guilty on both counts and was reported to the nearby Spanish Royal Guard.

Father LaRue ordered the mine to be concealed, working throughout the night to seal the entrance to the mine shafts, sealing their large cache of gold inside to be retrieved later. Before the sun rose, they moved their camp several miles down the mountain to further conceal the location of the mine.

When the soldiers arrived, they demanded to know where the gold came from. Padre LaRue and his monks refused to cooperate. After several hours of harsh treatment, Padre LaRue and several monks died. The Spanish soldiers searched for the mine to no avail and returned to Mesilla empty handed.

Treasure hunters have searched for the Lost Padre Mine for years. Some claim the mine was actually located in the Organ Mountains east of Las Cruces, or the Caballo Mountains near Truth or Consequences. Most, however, search in the San Andreas mountains. While clues have been found, no one has found gold...yet.

You can read the entire story in the March 3rd, 2012 edition of El Defensor Chieftain newspaper.

~Chapter 1 ~

Padre LaRue

The Mission of Santa María de las Cuevas stood as a beacon of Spanish influence in the rugged terrain of Chihuahua, New Spain. Its weathered stone walls rose from the arid landscape, a testament to the determination of the Franciscan missionaries who had established this outpost of faith decades earlier, following the expulsion of the Jesuits in 1767.

The year was 1797, and the mission had evolved significantly since its transfer to Franciscan control. The central church, with its simple yet elegant facade and sturdy bell tower, dominated the complex. Its bells, cast in a nearby foundry, rang out across the Chihuahuan desert, calling the faithful to prayer and marking the rhythms of mission life.

Surrounding the church, a series of low, adobe buildings formed a protective square. These housed workshops where Tarahumara and Conchos neophytes — indigenous converts — learned European crafts under the watchful eyes of the Franciscan friars. The air was filled with the sounds of industry: the clang of a blacksmith's hammer, the scraping of leather being tanned, the rhythmic thud of a loom weaving local wool.

In the mission's gardens, carefully tended rows of corn, beans, and chili peppers stretched towards the nearby hills. Peach and apple trees, introduced by the Spanish, provided welcome shade from the intense Chihuahuan sun. A complex system of irrigation channels, inspired by both Spanish and indigenous techniques, diverted precious water from the Conchos River to nourish every plant.

Beyond the cultivated fields, herds of cattle and goats grazed on the sparse vegetation of the semi-arid range. Vaqueros, many of them Tarahumara men who had embraced the horseback riding culture, kept a watchful eye for predators and Apache raiders, whose incursions had become more frequent in recent years.

Inside the mission walls, life moved to the steady rhythm of prayer and work. Franciscan friars in their brown robes moved purposefully through the courtyards, their sandaled feet stirring up small clouds of dust. Indigenous women, dressed in colorful blouses and long skirts, ground corn in stone metates, the steady scraping a constant backdrop to mission life.

Children darted between the buildings, their laughter a counterpoint to the solemn atmosphere. Some were orphans taken in by the mission, others the sons and daughters of converts. All were being raised in the Catholic faith, taught to read and write in Spanish, their native Tarahumara and Concho languages slowly fading with each passing generation.

As the sun began to set, painting the Chihuahuan sky in vibrant oranges and purples, the mission's inhabitants gathered in the church for evening prayers. The scent of local herbs used as incense filled the air, mingling with the earthy smell of adobe and the lingering aroma of the evening meal of beans, corn tortillas, and roasted goat.

In the fading light, the Mission of Santa María de las Cuevas stood as a microcosm of Spain's ambitions in the New World—a place where European and indigenous cultures collided and merged, creating something entirely new on the northern frontier of New Spain. Yet, as the 18th century drew to a close, winds of change were beginning to stir across the

Spanish colonies, winds that would soon challenge the very foundations of mission life in Chihuahua and beyond.

The sun beat down mercilessly on the adobe walls of the pueblo, its harsh rays painting the dusty streets in shades of gold and amber. Amidst the bustling life of the settlement, a young Mexican boy darted through the crowd, his bare feet kicking up small clouds of dust as he ran. He weaved between farmers tending to their crops, women haggling over produce at makeshift market stalls, and the occasional donkey laden with goods.

The child's eyes, wide with urgency, locked onto his target: Padre LaRue. The Spanish priest sat at a weathered wooden table in the shadow of a plastered statue, his fingers tracing the lines of scripture in the book before him. His dark brown robe, cinched at the waist by a rope from which dangled a simple wooden cross, stood out starkly against the sun-bleached surroundings.

"¡Padre, Padre!" the boy cried out in Spanish, his voice cracking with desperation as he skidded to a halt before the priest. "A soldier has arrived, and he's dying! He needs to see you immediately!"

Padre LaRue looked up from his text, his brow furrowing with concern as he took in the child's dirty face and torn clothes. "Take me to him, my son," he replied in Spanish, rising swiftly to his feet.

As they hurried through the pueblo, the sounds of daily life faded into a distant hum. The boy led the padre to a barn on the outskirts of the settlement, where a small crowd had already gathered. Women whispered among themselves, children peeked curiously from behind their mothers' skirts, and a few animals milled about, sensing the tension in the air.

There, propped against the barn's wall, lay a Spanish soldier. His uniform was caked with dirt and torn in several places, hinting at a recent and violent confrontation. But it was the dark stain spreading across his midsection that drew the eye – a testament to the gravity of his condition.

Padre LaRue approached the dying man, his steps measured and calm despite the urgency of the situation. He knelt beside the soldier, the hem of his robe settling in the dust. "My son," he said softly in Spanish, "what has happened to you?"

The soldier's eyes, glazed with pain, focused on the padre's face. His breath came in ragged gasps as he struggled to speak. "There is no time," he managed to rasp out. "I need to confess to you...what we have done!"

A flicker of something – curiosity, perhaps, or concern – passed across Padre LaRue's face. "Go ahead, my son," he urged gently. "What is your confession?"

With every ounce of energy, the soldiers leaned closer and whispered in Padre LaRue's ear. His hand trembling, the soldier then pressed something into the padre's palm. Their eyes met for a brief moment, a silent exchange passing between them. Then, with a final, shuddering breath, the soldier's body went limp, his secret dying with him.

Padre LaRue closed his eyes, whispering a quiet prayer for the departed soul. As he stood, he pulled back his hood, revealing a face weathered by sun and time. His gaze drifted to the vast expanse of desert stretching beyond the pueblo, as if searching for answers in the shimmering heat waves.

Abruptly, he turned on his heel and strode purposefully back toward his quarters, leaving the confused and curious onlookers behind.

"¡Padre!" the young boy called after him in Spanish. "What did he tell you?"

But Padre LaRue did not slow his pace or turn back. His mind was already racing, filled with the implications of what had just transpired. As he reached his humble abode, he pulled out a map and spread it across his table. His eyes traced the contours of the Franklin Mountains, a spark of excitement igniting within him.

Slowly, he opened his hand to reveal what the soldier had given him: a single gold coin, its surface gleaming despite the grime. With swift movements, he tucked the coin into a hidden pocket of his robe.

A smile played at the corners of his mouth as he called out, "Consuela, come here. We need to gather the flock and leave immediately!"

The sounds of hurried preparations filled the air, and Padre LaRue's mind whirled with possibilities. The dying soldier's confession had set something that promised adventure, danger, and perhaps untold riches.

The scorching sun beat down on Padre Larue as he squinted at the distant mountains. Behind him, the small band of settlers stirred restlessly, their few possessions packed onto creaking wooden carts. Little Consuela tugged at his rough wool robe.

"Padre, are we really leaving the mission?" her eyes wide with a mix of fear and excitement.

Larue knelt beside her, his weathered face creasing into a gentle smile. "Yes, my child. God has called us to journey north, to lands unknown."

The boy, barely older than Consuela, piped up. "But what of the Apache? They say terrible things..."

Larue raised a hand to quiet the murmurs of concern rippling through the group. "We go with faith as our shield," he proclaimed. "The Lord will guide us to a new home, far beyond these lands claimed by Spain."

With a deep breath, Padre Larue turned northward once more. "Vamos," he called out, his voice carrying over the dusty plain.

~ Chapter 2 ~

Wayne Braddock, Treasure Hunter

The television studio buzzed with activity, a hive of technicians, cameramen, and production assistants scurrying about their tasks. Under the harsh glare of studio lights, two figures sat center stage: Wayne Braddock, a weathered treasure hunter with graying hair, and Samantha Stone, the poised interviewer guiding their conversation.

Samantha, her professional smile never wavering, turned to address the camera. "And we're back in the studio with famed treasure hunter and adventurer Wayne Braddock. Thank you again for joining us."

Wayne nodded, his rugged attire of loose tie, dirty dress shoes, and a less than fashionable jacket over a long-sleeved shirt a stark contrast to Samantha's polished appearance. "Thank you again for having me," he replied, a hint of unease in his voice.

While the interview progressed, Wayne regaled Samantha with tales of his recent exploits, including a wild goose chase involving Billy the Kid. "I was just on the trails for what turned out to be a lead that Billy the Kid was in fact Pat Garrett!" Wayne chuckled, his eyes twinkling with the memory. "There was this notion that Garrett had schizophrenia and was playing both himself and the Billy the Kid character!"

Samantha raised an eyebrow, her skepticism evident. "Surely that was not the case."

"No, it turned out to be a false trail," Wayne admitted. "But I did uncover some manuscripts that got me a strong payday with the state historical society!"

The conversation took a more serious turn as Samantha probed into Wayne's less successful ventures. "But not all of your adventures have turned out so well, have they?" she asked, her tone carefully neutral.

Wayne shifted uncomfortably in his chair, the bravado of moments ago fading. "The Apache legend Cochise," he began hesitantly. "The tribal elders wanted me to find where Cochise was buried. I thought I was on a strong lead, when I got chased out by a tribal faction that didn't appreciate me disturbing their lands."

"What happened?" Samantha pressed, leaning forward slightly.

In a dramatic gesture, Wayne stood and lifted his shirt, revealing a jagged scar on his side. "The Indians shot me with an arrow!" he exclaimed, a mix of indignation and lingering fear in his voice.

"What happened then?" Samantha asked, her eyes widening at the sight of the scar.

Wayne sat back down, his bravado returning. "What do you think? I got the hell out of there!"

The interview began winding down, Samantha inquiring about Wayne's future plans. "So, what's next on the adventure bucket list?"

Wayne's eyes lit up momentarily. "Actually, I hear that Pancho Villa's lost treasure might be in Baja. Might be a good excuse to go to Cabo and take a look. So, who knows?!"

Samantha's next comment, however, struck a nerve. "It would seem that you may consider focusing more on paying work than vacations these days."

Wayne turned away from the camera, his expression darkening. The weight of financial struggles and fading glory seemed to settle on his shoulders, visible even to the casual observer.

Sensing the shift in mood, Samantha smoothly wrapped up the segment. "I'd like to thank our guest, Mr. Wayne Braddock, for visiting us today. We'll be back with more after this short break."

The cameras then cut away, Wayne remaining seated, lost in thought. The studio lights dimmed, but the harsh reality of his situation seemed to linger. Once a celebrated adventurer, he now found himself chasing increasingly far-fetched leads, his reputation tarnishing with each failed expedition. The scar on his side was a constant reminder of the dangers he faced, yet the thrill of the hunt still called to him.

Little did Wayne know that his next adventure was about to begin, one that would test his skills, challenge his beliefs, and perhaps offer a chance at redemption. As he left the studio that night, the echoes of Samantha's words rang in his ears, spurring him towards a decision that would change the course of his life forever.

In a dimly lit apartment, the flickering light of a television cast long shadows across the cluttered space. Padre Miguel Gonzalez, a Hispanic man with deep-set eyes and a face etched with lines of worry, sat motionless in an old armchair. His gaze was fixed on the screen, where Wayne Braddock's interview played out in technicolor contrast to the somber surroundings.

The room spoke volumes about its occupant. Religious artifacts adorned every available surface - ornate crosses hung on the walls, well-worn bibles lay open on side tables, and a priest's collar peeked out from beneath a pile of papers. It was clear that Padre Gonzalez was a man of faith, his calling evident in every corner of his humble abode.

Yet there was a tension in the air, a sense of unease that permeated the apartment. On the coffee table before him, alongside the religious texts and devotional items, lay a scattered array of bills and notices. Each bore the name of the Spanish mission where Gonzalez worked, their urgent red stamps a stark reminder of worldly concerns intruding on spiritual matters.

Padre Gonzalez stood before the weathered mirror in his sparse quarters, adjusting his clerical collar with trembling fingers. At fifty-three, his once-black hair had faded to a steely gray, matching the dullness he saw in his own eyes. Twenty-five years of service to the El Paso Catholic Church, and what did he have to show for it? A small office tucked away in the church's least-visited corridor and a congregation that barely remembered his name.

Gonzalez sighed, his shoulders sagging under the weight of unfulfilled ambitions. He had entered the priesthood with grand visions of making a difference, of leaving an indelible mark on the community. Instead, he found himself relegated to mundane tasks –

organizing bake sales, maintaining the church archives, and delivering uninspired sermons to dwindling Sunday crowds.

His colleagues, younger and more charismatic priests, seemed to effortlessly command respect and admiration. They led mission trips to far-flung corners of the world, spearheaded community outreach programs, and drew crowds with their impassioned homilies. Gonzalez watched from the sidelines, a bitter taste in his mouth that no amount of communion wine could wash away.

It wasn't that Gonzalez lacked faith or dedication. On the contrary, his devotion to the church was unwavering. But somewhere along the way, he had lost the spark that had once burned so brightly within him. His sermons, once filled with fire and conviction, had become rote recitations of scripture. His interactions with parishioners, once warm and engaging, had grown stilted and perfunctory.

Yet, beneath the veneer of resignation, a flame of ambition still flickered in Padre Gonzalez's heart. He yearned for an opportunity to prove his worth, to show his peers and superiors that he was capable of greatness. In quiet moments, he imagined himself making a groundbreaking historical discovery in the church archives, or brokering peace in a community dispute, or uncovering a long-lost religious artifact. Anything that would elevate him from obscurity to prominence.

But Gonzalez was a patient man. He knew that rushing into ill-conceived schemes would only invite ridicule and further damage his already tenuous standing. So he waited, biding his time, keeping his eyes and ears open for that one golden opportunity that would change everything.

As he made his way down the church corridor, ignored by the bustling younger priests and volunteers, Padre Gonzalez's lips curled into a small, secretive smile. They might overlook him now, but someday – someday soon, he hoped – they would all see. Miguel Gonzalez would make his mark, and the name they so easily forgot would be etched indelibly in the annals of their church's history.

Until then, he would wait, watch, and prepare. For Padre Gonzalez knew that destiny favored the prepared, and when his moment came, he would be ready to seize it with both hands.

Watching Wayne Braddock on the screen as he regaled the interviewer with tales of his treasure-hunting exploits, Padre Gonzalez reached for the whisky bottle at his side. He poured himself another measure, the amber liquid catching the light as it splashed into the glass. With a practiced motion, he brought the drink to his lips, his eyes never leaving the television.

Suddenly, something in the interview caught Gonzalez's attention. He leaned forward, his body tense with sudden focus. In one swift motion, he set his whisky glass down on top of the pile of bills, condensation from the glass slowly seeping into the paper beneath.

With trembling hands, Padre Gonzalez reached for a nearby notepad and pen. As Wayne Braddock's name left the interviewer's lips, Gonzalez scribbled it down, his handwriting urgent and messy. The pen dug into the paper, leaving deep indentations as if trying to etch the name into his memory as well as the page.

The padre sat back, staring at the name he had written. His eyes darted between the television and the notepad, a mix of emotions playing across his face - hope, fear, desperation, and perhaps a touch of guilt. It was clear that Wayne Braddock's words had stirred something within him, awakening a long-buried secret or a desperate plan.

The interview concluded and the program shifted to commercials. Padre Gonzalez remained frozen in his seat. The sounds of the television faded into background noise as his mind raced with possibilities. In the soft glow of the screen, his eyes took on a determined glint.

Whatever connection existed between the treasure hunter on the screen and the struggling priest in this small apartment, it was clear that Padre Gonzalez saw Wayne Braddock as more than just an entertaining interviewee. To him, this man represented something far more significant - perhaps a solution to his problems, or maybe a key to unlocking a mystery that had long haunted him.

Sensing the night wear on, Padre Gonzalez remained vigilant, his thoughts churning with plans and prayers in equal measure. The world outside his apartment continued its nocturnal rhythm, unaware that in this small, cluttered room, the first threads of an extraordinary adventure were beginning to weave themselves together.

Wayne Braddock loosened his tie as he stepped out of the studio, the bright lights and probing questions of the interview already fading from his mind. His phone buzzed — a message from Elizabeth.

"Saw you on TV. You looked good. Dinner still on?"

He smiled, a warmth spreading through his chest. After years of fleeting romances and spectacular breakups splashed across gossip rags, Elizabeth felt different. Real.

Wayne's thoughts drifted to their upcoming dinner. He'd promised to cook this time — a simple pasta dish he'd been practicing in secret. It wasn't much, but it was a start.

Wayne pulled up to his home, and he paused before getting out. He took a deep breath, steeling himself. "Don't mess this up," he muttered. "Not like the others."

Inside, he found Elizabeth curled up on the couch, reading. She looked up, her smile genuine. "Hey, superstar. Ready to impress me with your culinary skills?"

Wayne grinned back, pushing aside his fears. "Prepare to be amazed," he said, heading for the kitchen. For once, he wasn't acting. This felt like a scene he wanted to play for the rest of his life.

~ Chapter 3 ~
El Paso

The morning sun filtered through the curtains, casting a warm glow over Wayne Braddock's bedroom. Wayne stirred, gradually becoming aware of his beautiful younger girlfriend Elizabeth lying beside him, her arm draped possessively across his chest. The peaceful moment was shattered by the shrill ring of a telephone.

Wayne Braddock lay sprawled on his bed, staring at the ceiling fan as it lazily spun above him. At 45, the lines etching his weathered face told stories of adventures in far-flung corners of the world. His salt-and-pepper hair, perpetually tousled, splayed across the pillow, giving him the appearance of a man who had just returned from some grand expedition. In many ways,

23

that was exactly the image Wayne had carefully cultivated over the years.

To the outside world, Wayne Braddock was a daring treasure hunter who fearlessly delved into ancient tombs and deciphered cryptic maps to unearth priceless artifacts. His name graced the covers of adventure magazines, and his exploits were recounted in hushed, awe-struck tones in the dimly lit bars frequented by wannabe explorers.

But as Wayne's gaze traced the cracks in the ceiling plaster, he felt the familiar pang of dissonance between his public persona and his private reality. The truth was far less glamorous than the tales that circulated about him.

For every successful find, there were a dozen expeditions that ended in frustration and near-bankruptcy. The golden idol from Peru that made headlines? It barely covered the cost of the expedition and the bribes needed to get it out of the country. The lost city in the Cambodian jungle? A fascinating discovery, sure, but one that yielded more academic papers than actual treasure.

Wayne absently fingered the scar on his left hand – a souvenir from a close call with a booby trap in an Egyptian tomb. He chuckled ruefully, remembering how he'd embellished that story for the press, turning a simple cut into a death-defying escape.

The truth was, Wayne Braddock was addicted to the thrill of the hunt. It wasn't about the money – though God knew he could use some. It was about the rush of piecing together ancient clues, the excitement of setting foot where no one had tread for centuries, the intoxicating possibility that this time, this expedition would be the one that changed everything. But with each passing year, the pressure mounted. The mortgage on the house was three months behind.

Yet, even as the weight of his responsibilities pressed down on him, Wayne couldn't bring himself to give up the life. He was a treasure hunter true and true. It was who he was, who he'd always been. The idea of settling for a normal 9-to-5 job felt like a death sentence to his spirit.

So, he pushed on, chasing the next big score, convinced that it was just around the corner. He took bigger risks, ventured into more dangerous territories, always with the hope that this would be the find that secured his legacy and his family's future.

Wayne gently tried to extricate himself from Elizabeth's embrace, eliciting a sleepy moan of protest. "What the hell is that?!" she mumbled, burrowing deeper into the pillows.

"My landline," Wayne replied, stretching to reach the phone on the nightstand.

25

Elizabeth, now more awake, rolled her eyes. "You should get a cell phone."

Wayne chuckled, a hint of melancholy in his voice. "You sound like someone else I know."

Watching Wayne fumbled for the phone, Elizabeth sat up, the sheet falling away to reveal her partial nudity. "She sounds like a smart girl," she quipped, reaching down to retrieve her scattered clothes from the floor.

Wayne's eyes couldn't help but linger on her form for a moment before he answered the call. "Hello?"

On the other end of the line, a voice with a distinct Hispanic accent responded, "Yes, am I speaking to Mr. Wayne Braddock?"

Wayne's attention was split between the caller and the distracting sight of his companion dressing. "Uh, yeah, it is. Who is this?"

"I am Padre Gonzalez, a pastor in El Paso," the voice explained. "I saw your TV interview."

Wayne's brow furrowed in confusion. "Oh yeah? Thanks, but I'm really not that much of a religious person."

The padre's response caught Wayne off guard. "No, I don't think you understand. I'd like to invite you to my church and discuss the possibility of seeking some lost valuables taken from the church long ago."

Wayne paused; his interest piqued despite his initial skepticism. "El Paso?"

"Yes," Padre Gonzalez confirmed.

A slow smile spread across Wayne's face as he reached for a pen, his mind already racing with possibilities. The prospect of a new adventure, especially one involving lost church valuables, was too tempting to ignore.

Wayne furiously jotted down the details as his slim female companion finished dressing, casting him a curious glance. "Another job?" she asked, a mix of resignation and excitement in her voice.

Wayne nodded, covering the mouthpiece of the phone. "Might be. El Paso."

She smiled, leaning down to plant a kiss on his cheek. "Well, don't get shot with any more arrows, okay?"

Elizabeth gathered her things and slipped out of the bedroom. Wayne turned his full attention back to the call. "Alright, Padre," he said, his voice taking on a more professional tone. "Tell me more about these lost valuables."

While Padre Gonzalez began to explain, Wayne's eyes drifted to the bedside table where a framed photo stood. It showed a younger version of himself, grinning broadly next to an older man with a weathered face and kind eyes. The inscription read: "To Wayne, may you always find the greatest treasures in life. Love, Dad."

For a moment, Wayne's expression softened, a mix of nostalgia and determination crossing his features. Then, refocusing on the padre's words, he began to take notes, the thrill of a new hunt already coursing through his veins.

Little did Wayne know that this seemingly routine call would set in motion a chain of events that would challenge everything he thought he knew about treasure hunting, faith, and his own past. As he listened to Padre Gonzalez's tale, the seeds of an extraordinary adventure were being sown, one that would take Wayne Braddock on a journey far beyond anything he had experienced before.

The scorching Texas sun beat down on the tarmac as Wayne Braddock's plane touched down at El Paso International Airport. The desert landscape stretched out beyond the runways, a stark contrast to the lush greenery he'd left behind.

Inside the terminal, Wayne made his way through the crowds, his weathered leather bag slung over one shoulder. He pushed his sunglasses up onto his head as he exited the baggage claim area, squinting against the bright sunlight that flooded through the glass doors.

Before he could get his bearings, a blur of motion caught his eye. A young woman with long dark hair came rushing towards him, her face lit up with a brilliant smile.

"Wayne!" she called out, throwing her arms around him in an enthusiastic embrace.

Caught off guard but pleasantly surprised, Wayne returned the hug, a genuine smile spreading across his face. "Hey Selena, good to see you," he said warmly, the tension of travel melting away in the face of such a heartfelt welcome.

It was Selena Martinez, the daughter of a longtime friend. Selena pulled back, her eyes sparkling with excitement. "You too," she replied, then gestured towards the parking lot. "I'm parked over there."

As they walked side by side towards the short-term parking area, Wayne couldn't help but marvel at how much Selena had grown since he'd last seen her. She'd been just a teenager then, all gangly limbs and braces. Now she moved with the confidence of a young woman coming into her own.

"So, how's your mother?" Wayne asked, genuine concern in his voice. "I was surprised when you called instead of her."

Selena's smile faltered slightly. "She's... okay. Busy with work, you know how it is."

Wayne nodded, sensing there was more to the story but not wanting to push. "Well, I appreciate you coming to pick me up. It's been too long since I've been down this way."

Selena's car was a beat-up but well-loved sedan. She turned to face him. "Wayne, I know you're here on business, but... I hope we'll have some time to catch up. There's a lot I want to talk to you about."

The seriousness in her tone caught Wayne's attention. He studied her face for a moment, seeing a mix of hope and worry in her eyes. "Of course, kiddo," he said softly, using the old nickname without thinking. "We'll make time."

The two got into the car and pulled out of the parking lot. Wayne's mind raced with questions. What had brought him to El Paso wasn't just the promise of lost church valuables, but also the chance to reconnect with old friends - and perhaps, he realized, to face some ghosts from his past.

The city sprawled out before them, a mix of modern buildings and historic architecture, all set against the backdrop of the Franklin Mountains. Wayne couldn't shake the feeling that this trip was going to be about much more than just another treasure hunt.

Selena navigated the busy streets, occasionally glancing at Wayne with a mixture of admiration and nervousness. He found himself wondering what secrets lay hidden in this border town - and what price he might have to pay to uncover them.

The El Paso sun beat down mercilessly as Selena's car wound through the city streets. Inside, the air conditioning struggled against the heat, creating a cocoon of coolness that contrasted sharply with the tension building between the two occupants.

"So, what brings you to Hell Paso?" Selena asked, her eyes fixed on the road ahead.

Wayne smirked, leaning back in his seat. "Come on, you know I came to see you."

Selena's laughter filled the car, tinged with a hint of bitterness. "Yeah right. When was the last time you ever came to visit me?"

"Including this time?" Wayne quipped, earning an eye roll from Selena.

"Yeah, well don't expect me to be driving you around everywhere," she retorted.

Wayne raised an eyebrow. "Why not?"

Selena's response came quickly, a mix of defiance and pride. "I got a new boyfriend, and I don't think he'd like seeing me with some old dude."

Wayne paused, considering his next words carefully. "I'm also here for a treasure hunt."

"I knew it!" Selena exclaimed, a triumphant note in her voice. "You didn't come to see me!"

"Two birds, sweetheart," Wayne replied, trying to smooth things over.

Selena gasped in mock shock. "Whatever."

A moment of uncomfortable silence fell between them before Wayne spoke again, his voice softer. "How's your Mom, really?"

Selena's grip on the steering wheel tightened. "We get by as best we can, even with an awful economy. But, you could call yourself and find out, mister 'I'm too busy to pick up my old fifty's broke phone'!"

Wayne winced at the accusation, guilt washing over him. Trying to change the subject, he circled back to an earlier topic. "So, boyfriend, huh?"

"Uh huh," Selena confirmed, a hint of pride creeping into her voice. "Big, strong, tough mofo."

Wayne couldn't resist the opportunity for a little teasing. "Good, so he can drive you around and I'll borrow this car."

"That's not what I meant!" Selena protested, but there was a hint of amusement in her voice.

Wayne found himself studying Selena's profile. She'd grown so much since he'd last seen her, no longer the little girl who used to beg for stories of his adventures. Now she was a young woman with her own life, her own challenges, and apparently, her own tough boyfriend.

The familiar landmarks of El Paso slid by outside the windows, bringing with them a flood of memories for Wayne. He'd spent a lot of time in this city years ago, working with Selena's father on various projects. It had been like a second home once.

"Look, Selena," Wayne began, his voice serious. "I know I haven't been around much, and I'm sorry for that. But I'm here now, and not just for some treasure hunt. I want to help if I can."

Selena glanced at him, her expression softening slightly. "Mom's spending all her time at the church, barely coming home."

As they approached their destination, Wayne felt a mix of anticipation and apprehension. He was back in El Paso, about to dive into a new adventure, but this time the stakes felt higher. This wasn't just about finding lost valuables; it was about helping old friends and maybe, just maybe, finding a bit of redemption along the way.

"We're almost there," Selena announced, pulling up to a modest church. "You ready for this?"

Wayne took a deep breath, steeling himself for whatever lay ahead. "As ready as I'll ever be, kiddo. Stay here, I'll be back shortly."

Wayne stepped out of the car into the sweltering heat. His boots crunched on the gravel as he walked away from the idling car. He could feel Selena's eyes boring into his back, but he didn't turn around. Couldn't face her. Not after what he'd just done.

Maybe somewhere along the way, he'd figure out how to be a better friend — if Selena ever gave him another chance.

~Chapter 4~
The Pastor's Offer

The night had settled over El Paso like a heavy blanket, broken only by the soft glow of streetlights and the silver sheen of a full moon hanging low in the sky. Against this backdrop, the Spanish mission stood as a silent sentinel, its weathered walls bathed in gentle illumination.

Wayne's footsteps echoed in the empty courtyard as he approached the heavy wooden doors of the mission. Wayne paused for a moment, taking in the intricate carvings that adorned the entrance, before raising his hand to knock firmly.

The sound reverberated through the night, and for a long moment, there was no response. Just as Wayne was considering knocking again, he heard the faint scrape of a bolt being drawn back. The door creaked open a fraction, revealing a sliver of shadowed interior.

"Who is it?" a voice called out, tinged with wariness.

Wayne leaned closer to the gap. "I am Wayne Braddock. I'm supposed to meet a priest named Gonzalez?"

There was a sharp intake of breath from the other side of the door, and suddenly it swung wide open. Before Wayne could react, a hand shot out, grabbing his arm and yanking him inside with surprising strength. He stumbled across the threshold as Padre Gonzalez - for it could be no one else - peered out into the night, his eyes darting back and forth as if searching for unseen watchers.

Satisfied that they were alone, Gonzalez slammed the door shut, the sound echoing through the cavernous interior of the mission. Wayne found himself in a dimly lit entryway, surrounded by the scent of old wood and candle wax.

"Padre Gonzalez, I presume?" Wayne said, trying to inject some levity into the tense atmosphere.

The priest turned to face him, and Wayne was struck by the man's appearance. Padre Gonzalez was older than he had expected, with deep lines etched into his face and a shock of silver hair. But it was his eyes that caught Wayne's attention - they burned with an intensity that spoke of both fear and determination.

"Mr. Braddock," Gonzalez said, his voice low and urgent. "I'm glad you've come, but we must be careful. There are those who would not look kindly on our meeting."

Wayne's eyebrows shot up. "What exactly have I walked into here, Padre?"

Gonzalez glanced nervously at the door once more before gesturing for Wayne to follow him deeper into the mission. "Come. We have much to discuss, and little time. The fate of more than just lost valuables hangs in the balance."

They moved through the shadowy corridors of the ancient mission. Wayne couldn't shake the feeling that he had just stepped into something far more dangerous and complex than he had anticipated. The treasure hunter in him thrilled at the prospect of a real mystery, but another part - the part that remembered the warmth of Selena's welcome and the unspoken worries in her eyes - warned him to tread carefully.

Whatever secrets Padre Gonzalez was about to reveal, Wayne had a feeling they would change everything. As they entered what appeared to be the priest's study, lit only by a few flickering candles, Wayne steeled himself for what was to come.

"Alright, Padre," he said, settling into a worn leather chair. "I'm all ears. What's this all about?"

Padre Gonzalez closed the study door with a soft click, then turned to face Wayne, his expression grave. "Mr. Braddock, what I'm about to tell you may sound unbelievable, but I assure you, it is all too real. It begins with a legend - the legend of the Lost Padre Mine..."

"We are facing troubled times here in El Paso," the pastor said, his voice low and tinged with worry. He gestured to a nearby bench. "Please, sit down."

Wayne settled onto the worn wooden seat, not helping but notice the large Jesus statue in the background, eerily similar to the one he'd seen in old photographs of Padre LaRue's time. The air was thick with the scent of candle wax and old stone, creating an atmosphere of timeless secrets.

Pastor Gonzalez lowered himself onto the bench next to Wayne, his face etched with lines of concern. "There is corruption in the city, both from the US and from Juarez drug cartels. My congregation is not exempt from the terrors that are happening here."

As the priest began his tale, Wayne leaned forward, his senses alert. Outside, the moon continued its silent vigil over El Paso, unaware of the storm that was about to break in this quiet corner of the desert night.

Wayne kept thinking of how the interior of the Spanish mission was a world apart from the night outside. Flickering candles cast dancing shadows across weathered stone walls, their warm glow barely illuminating the vast space. Wayne noticed a cane leaning against the wall, which Gonzalez grabbed, revealing a pronounced limp as he moved.

Wayne, feeling a mix of impatience and curiosity, cut to the chase. "Yeah... so, about this treasure?"

The pastor's eyes widened at Wayne's abruptness, but he pressed on. "There are many tales of our ancestor, a Padre LaRue, as well as his inspiration, Fray Garcia de San Francisco. LaRue was a missionary back in the 18th Century who came across a vast fortune somewhere in this area. I think that, should you find this treasure, I can use it to make things better here."

Wayne couldn't hide his skepticism. "LaRue hid the missing Spanish treasure. Seriously?"

Gonzalez's face flushed with embarrassment, but his voice remained earnest. "I would search for this myself, but as you can see, I am not in the strongest of conditions. I fear that I cannot completely trust the people here either. But you, you are not tainted by ghost stories of haunted treasures. You are not deterred by the dangers of the drug cartel. And, to be frank, I think you may use a little more success these days!"

Wayne stood, ready to dismiss the whole affair as another wild goose chase. But Gonzalez's next move stopped him in his tracks. The pastor produced a gleaming gold coin, holding it up to catch the candlelight. "Please! This treasure exists! I know it does! I need your help finding it."

Wayne's eyes locked onto the coin, his treasure hunter's instincts kicking in. "I get twenty percent of what is found," he said, his voice steady.

"Agreed," Gonzalez replied without hesitation.

"And that percentage starts with this coin," Wayne added, a hint of a smile playing at the corners of his mouth.

Gonzalez begrudgingly handed over the coin. Wayne felt its weight in his palm – the weight of history, of possibility. "Like I said, LaRue and Spanish treasure! Where should I begin?"

The pastor's excitement was palpable as he hurried over to the Jesus statue. From its base, he retrieved a cloth, handling it with reverence. "This has been known as a clue left by LaRue many years ago. Use this to find the treasure."

As Padre Gonzalez handed the cloth to Wayne, he unfolded it to reveal a medallion. Wayne examined the cloth, his mind already racing with potential leads and connections. He then turned to the medallion, noticing that it was silver with segmented gaps that created a tree design. Wayne wondered what a tree and a rag had to do with missing treasure. As he looked up, he found Gonzalez smiling at him, hope shining in the older man's eyes.

In that moment, surrounded by flickering candlelight and centuries of history, Wayne felt the familiar thrill of a new adventure taking hold. But beneath the excitement, a sobering thought nagged at him: if this treasure was real, and if it truly could help the people of El Paso, then the stakes were higher than any hunt he'd undertaken before.

Wayne carefully folded the cloth and pocketed both the medallion and the coin, making a silent promise – to himself, to Pastor Gonzalez, and to the memory of Padre LaRue. He would unravel this mystery, no matter where it led him.

"Alright, Pastor," Wayne said, his voice filled with determination. "Let's see where this trail takes us."

With a nod of gratitude, Pastor Gonzalez began to share everything he knew about the legend of the Lost Padre Mine. As the night deepened outside the mission walls, Wayne Braddock found himself drawn ever deeper into a centuries-old mystery that would challenge not just his skills as a treasure hunter, but his very understanding of faith, history, and the power of long-buried secrets.

Watching Wayne walk back to his car, Padre Gonzalez noticed a young girl sitting in the passenger seat. He wondered who this Latina lady was, and whether he may have inadvertently placed her in danger. Was the risk of placing others in harm's way worth the potential gains in discovering the lost treasure? Padre Gonzalez decided that he would pray on that notion, and see what divine guidance would come to him.

~ Chapter 5 ~
The Statue of Saint Francisco

The hotel room had become Wayne's fortress of solitude, a cluttered shrine to his obsession with the Lost Padre Mine. Days had blended into one another as he pored over every scrap of information, his beard growing unkempt, a testament to his single-minded focus.

The walls were covered with corkboards, a chaotic tapestry of clues and connections. The mysterious cloth hung at the center, surrounded by a web of photographs, reports, and scribbled notes. A fabric analysis report sat next to a picture of the Franklin Mountains, the letter "A" circled emphatically. Images of kapok trees mingled with architectural sketches

43

from Trost. A statue of Fray Garcia de San Francisco watched over it all, a silent sentinel to Wayne's frustration.

Outside, Selena sat in her boyfriend's car, contemplating her family situation. At 22, she was caught in the limbo between youth and adulthood, her mind a tumultuous mix of hopes, fears, and uncertainties.

She thought of the acceptance letter from a local college that lay on her desk, its crisp edges a stark contrast to the cluttered mess of her room. Next to it, a framed photo of her and Miguel, her boyfriend of three years. Two paths, two futures, both terrifying in their own way.

Selena's fingers absently traced the outline of the turquoise pendant around her neck – a gift from her abuela, a reminder of her heritage. As a Mexican American, Selena had always felt caught between two worlds. Too Mexican for some, not Mexican enough for others. It was a tightrope she'd been walking her entire life, and now, faced with major life decisions, that cultural tug-of-war felt stronger than ever.

She thought of her mother, María, and felt a pain in her chest. On the surface, María was the perfect picture of a successful immigrant – hardworking, always smiling, the backbone of their family. But Selena had seen the cracks in that facade. The way her mother's smile didn't quite reach her eyes anymore. The quiet sighs when she
44

thought no one was listening. The half-empty bottle of antidepressants hidden behind the aspirin in the medicine cabinet.

Was that her future? The thought sent a chill down Selena's spine. She loved Miguel, she truly did. He was kind, stable, and his family adored her. Marriage to him promised a life of comfort and security. But was that enough? The idea of settling down in their small town, of possibly falling into the same quiet desperation as her mother, terrified her.

Yet the alternative – pursuing her dreams of becoming a biomedical engineer – seemed equally daunting. It meant leaving behind everything familiar, venturing into a world where she'd be one of the few Latinas in her field. The imposter syndrome that had plagued her throughout college whispered insidiously in her ear. Was she really smart enough? Did she belong in that world?

Selena sat up, hugging her knees to her chest. She was smart – she knew that objectively. Her perfect GPA and the stack of academic awards gathering dust on her bookshelf were testament to that. But intelligence alone wasn't enough to quiet the doubts that gnawed at her.

What did she want from life? The safe, familiar path with Miguel? Or the uncertain, potentially lonely road of academic pursuits? Was there a way to have both, or was she destined to sacrifice one dream for another?

Selena's mind whirled with possibilities and fears. She thought of her younger cousins, how they looked up to her as the first in the family to go to college. She thought of her abuela's proud smile at her graduation. She thought of Miguel's warm embrace and the future he promised.

Selena sighed, running a hand through her hair. The weight of her decisions felt almost crushing. But beneath the fear and uncertainty, a small spark of excitement flickered. Her future was unwritten, full of possibilities. Whether she chose love or career, stayed or left, she had the power to shape her own destiny.

Selena made a quiet promise to herself. Whatever path she chose, she would forge it on her own terms. She would find a way to honor her heritage, pursue her passions, and create a life that was uniquely, unequivocally her own. The "how" of it all was still a mystery, but for the first time in a long while, Selena felt a glimmer of hope for what tomorrow might bring.

When a knock at the door interrupted Wayne's brooding, he almost ignored it. But something compelled him to answer, and he found Selena standing there, a breath of fresh air in his stale environment.

"So how goes the hunt, Mr. Wayne?" she asked, breezing past him into the room.

Wayne grunted, "Shouldn't you be in school or something?"

Selena's response was tinged with a bitterness that Wayne couldn't miss. "Would if I could afford it. Until then, I get to spend my free time with you!"

"I thought you had a boyfriend. Go bother him!" Wayne retorted, but there was no real heat in his words.

Selena ignored his grumpiness, her eyes scanning the room with genuine interest. "Anyways, what are you up to?"

Wayne sighed, gesturing to the cloth on the wall. "I'm stuck on this clue. This cloth wrapped this necklace," he said, holding up the item in question. "I had the cloth analyzed, and the material is made from the kapok tree. The necklace is also a tree, presumably a kapok. I don't know, there's something there."

"Yeah, interesting," Selena mused. "Have you thought of googling some of this stuff?"

"Google?" Wayne's confusion was evident.

Selena sighed, a mix of exasperation and fondness in her voice. "I'm no expert, but don't you need to get out and find clues or something? If this treasure is out there, shouldn't you be out there?"

Wayne's sarcasm kicked in. "Maybe I can just go to the Gold mine marked 'LaRue's stash'?"

"Yeah, maybe..." Selena wrinkled her nose. "Now don't take this the wrong way. But it smells in here! You need to get out, and I mean now!"

Wayne's gaze drifted to the picture of de Francisco, and something in his mind clicked. "That might not be a bad idea," he muttered, a spark of excitement returning to his eyes.

Without another word, Wayne grabbed his jacket and headed for the door. Selena barely had time to react as he snatched her car keys from her hand.

"You're welcome!" she called after him, a smile playing on her lips as she watched him rush off, reinvigorated by the prospect of action.

Wayne drove through the streets of El Paso, his mind racing with possibilities. The stagnation of the hotel room fell away, replaced by the thrill of the hunt. He realized that Selena was right – the answers he sought weren't going to be found in fabric analyses and old photographs. They were out there, hidden in the landscape and history of El Paso itself.

His first stop would be the statue of Fray Garcia de San Francisco. Maybe there, in the shadow of the man who inspired Padre LaRue, he would find the next piece of the puzzle. As he navigated the city streets, Wayne felt a renewed sense of purpose. The treasure was out there, and he was determined to find it – not just for himself, but for Pastor Gonzalez, for Selena, and for all those in El Paso who needed hope in these troubled times.

The hunt for the Lost Padre Mine was about to enter a new phase, and Wayne Braddock was ready to face whatever challenges lay ahead. As he pulled up to the site of the statue, he took a deep breath, steeling himself for the adventure to come. "Alright, Padre LaRue," he muttered, stepping out of the car. "Let's see what secrets you've been hiding all these years."

The bustling streets of downtown El Paso faded into background noise as Wayne Braddock stood before the imposing statue of Fray Garcia de San Francisco. The midday sun beat down mercilessly, casting sharp shadows across the weathered bronze figure.

Wayne circled the statue, his eyes darting from one detail to another, searching for anything that might connect to the enigmatic cloth and the legend of the Lost Padre Mine. He stepped back, taking in the full view, then moved in close, examining every crevice and contour.

Wayne studied the statue, his attention drawn to the way the sun's rays interacted with the sculpture. The left hand, raised in a gesture of blessing, cast a distinct shadow across the pole held in the right hand.

Something about this interplay of light and shadow nagged at Wayne's instincts.

Wayne's gaze dropped to the base of the pole, where an engraving caught his eye. It was a stylized representation of a kapok tree – the same tree that had been so central to his research back in the hotel room. Wayne's pulse quickened. This couldn't be a coincidence.

Glancing at his watch, he noted the time: 1358 hours. Wayne settled onto a nearby bench, pulling an apple from his bag. As he ate, his eyes never left the statue, watching as the sun's position shifted ever so slowly across the sky.

Minutes ticked by, stretching into hours. Wayne barely noticed the passersby, some of whom cast curious glances at the scruffy man so intently focused on the old statue. His watch beeped softly as it hit 1659 – 4:59 PM.

In that moment, Wayne's attention snapped back to the statue. The shadow cast by the hovering hand had shifted, now falling directly over the letter "N" on the pole. Wayne's eyes widened as he registered the word "North" engraved on the statue's base.

He stood abruptly, turning to face north. There, rising majestically in the distance, stood a unique section of the Franklin Mountains. A chill ran down Wayne's spine despite the lingering heat of the day.

"1659," he muttered to himself, recalling the date he'd seen on the back of the cloth. "It's not just a year. It's a time. And a direction."

The pieces were starting to fall into place. The kapok tree, the specific time, the cardinal direction – all of it pointed towards the mountains looming on the horizon. Wayne felt a surge of excitement, the kind he hadn't experienced in years. This was a real lead, a tangible connection between the centuries-old mystery and the present day.

Wayne knew his next steps. He needed to explore the Franklin Mountains, to find whatever marker or landmark Padre LaRue might have left behind over 300 years ago. But he also knew he couldn't rush in blindly. The mountains were vast, and if the drug cartels Pastor Gonzalez had mentioned were involved, the danger was very real. He needed to plan, to gather supplies, and perhaps most importantly, to share his discovery with someone he could trust.

Wayne's thoughts turned to Selena. Despite his initial gruffness, he had to admit that her prodding had led him to this breakthrough. Maybe it was time to bring her into the hunt more fully. After all, this was her home, her history. And if the legends were true, the treasure could change the lives of people like her.

Wayne made his way back to Selena's borrowed car, his mind racing with possibilities and plans. The hunt for the Lost Padre Mine was no longer a vague quest based on ancient legends. It was a real, tangible mystery unfolding before him, with clues hidden in plain sight across El Paso.

"Alright, Padre LaRue," Wayne said softly as he started the car, casting one last glance at the statue of Fray Garcia de San Francisco. "Let's see what other secrets you've left for us to find."

With renewed purpose, Wayne headed towards into the heart of the Franklin Mountains.

~ Chapter 6 ~

Wyler's Tramway

The desert landscape blurred past as Wayne drove Selena's car along US Highway 54. His eyes, sharp despite the fatigue of days spent poring over clues, caught sight of a sign for the Wyler Tramway near George Wilson Road. A small smile played at the corners of his mouth as he made the turn. This was it - the path to the Franklin Mountains, and hopefully, to the next piece of the puzzle.

The parking lot of the Wyler Tramway was relatively quiet, a few tourists milling about as Wayne stepped out of the car. He stretched, his joints popping after the drive, and made his way to the ticket booth. The attendant gave him a curious look - Wayne knew he must look a sight, unshaven and bleary-eyed - but handed over a pass without comment.

Wayne boarded the tram. He felt a mixture of anticipation and trepidation. The cabin began its ascent, and he pressed his face to the window, watching as El Paso grew smaller below him. The Franklin Mountains loomed larger with each passing moment, their rugged beauty a stark contrast to the sprawling city at their feet.

Wayne's mind raced as the tram climbed higher. What would he find at the top? Would the clues from the statue of Fray Garcia de San Francisco lead him to the next step in unraveling the mystery of the Lost Padre Mine? Or was this just another dead end in a long line of disappointments?

The tram reached the station at the summit, and Wayne stepped out onto the observation deck. The view was breathtaking - El Paso and Ciudad Juárez spread out before him, two cities straddling an international border, their fates intertwined despite the barriers between them.

"You will never find a more wretched hive of scum and villainy," Wayne muttered to himself, paraphrasing an old movie line as he gazed down at the cities. But there was no real venom in his words - just a weary acknowledgment of the complex realities that had brought him to this point.

Tearing his eyes away from the vista, Wayne turned his attention to his surroundings. The observation deck was dotted with tourists taking photos and enjoying the view, but Wayne's gaze was searching for something else - any sign, any marker that might connect to Padre LaRue's centuries-old trail.

Not seeing anything immediately obvious, Wayne decided to explore further. He noticed a small gift shop and headed inside, hoping that perhaps among the touristy trinkets and postcards, he might find some local lore or historical information that could prove useful.

The gift shop was a cluttered space, filled with the usual tourist trinkets - postcards, t-shirts, and miniature replicas of the Franklin Mountains. But Wayne's trained eye was searching for something more substantial, something that might connect to the trail he was following.

As he browsed the shelves, Wayne's mind wandered back to Selena and Pastor Gonzalez. He felt a pang of guilt for not sharing his discoveries with them before rushing up here. But he also knew that sometimes in treasure hunting, you had to follow your instincts in the moment.

"Alright, Padre LaRue," Wayne murmured as he picked up a book on local history. "What secrets did you hide up here in these mountains? And more importantly, why?"

Flipping through the pages, Wayne couldn't shake the feeling that he was on the verge of something big. The clues were coming together, but the bigger picture was still frustratingly out of reach. Whatever Padre LaRue had hidden all those years ago, it was clear that uncovering it would take more than just solving a few riddles.

As he moved through the cramped aisles, a faded photograph on the wall caught his attention. It showed the wreckage of a plane, sprawled across the rugged terrain of the mountains. Wayne leaned in closer, his eyes narrowing as he took in the details.

The crash, according to the information beneath the photo, had occurred in 1953 - six years before the tramway was built. But what really caught Wayne's attention was a detail that seemed oddly out of place: a kapok tree edited into the background of the crashed plane.

Wayne's pulse quickened. The kapok tree had been a recurring symbol in his investigation, from the fabric of the mysterious cloth to the engraving on the statue of Fray Garcia de San Francisco. Its presence in this old photograph couldn't be a coincidence.

Turning to the store clerk, a bored-looking teenager, Wayne asked, "Where was this crash?"

The clerk looked up from his phone, confused. "What?"

Wayne pointed to the picture on the wall. "That one."

Recognition dawned on the clerk's face. "Oh, the bomber crash. Yeah, take the trail outside, you can see the wreckage. What's left of it, anyways."

Wayne nodded, already heading for the door. "Thanks," he called over his shoulder.

Wayne stepped back out onto the observation deck, his mind was racing. A plane crash from over half a century ago shouldn't have any connection to a centuries-old Spanish treasure. And yet, the presence of the kapok tree in that photo felt significant.

Wayne scanned the area, quickly locating the trailhead the clerk had mentioned. It was a rough path, winding its way along the mountainside. He checked his supplies - water, a small first aid kit, his notebook. It would have to do.

Wayne couldn't shake the feeling that he was on the verge of something big. The clues were coming together in unexpected ways, linking the distant past with more recent history. The sun was lower in the sky now, casting long shadows across the rugged terrain. Wayne picked his way carefully along the trail, his eyes constantly scanning for any sign of the crash site - or any other markers that might relate to Padre LaRue's treasure.

"What's your game, Padre?" Wayne muttered as he hiked. "A Spanish missionary, a centuries-old treasure, and now a 1950s plane crash? How does it all fit together?"

The trail grew steeper, and Wayne's breathing became more labored. But he pressed on, driven by the thrill of the hunt and the tantalizing promise of answers just beyond his reach.

The terrain was rugged, loose rocks shifting under his feet as he made his way along the mountainside. The city of El Paso sprawled below, a tapestry of lights beginning to twinkle as dusk approached.

Wayne suddenly found himself facing an unexpected sight. There, on the east side of the Franklin Mountains, a giant "A" stood out starkly against the rocky landscape. Constructed of large white painted rocks, it was impossible to miss – a human-made landmark in this natural setting.

Wayne paused, his brow furrowing as he took in the sight. "Now what's this all about?" he muttered to himself, recalling the "A" he had seen highlighted on the map back in his hotel room.

Intrigued, he made his way towards the clearing filled with white rocks. Standing in the center of the "A",

Wayne slowly turned in a circle, taking in the view from this unique vantage point. The setting sun cast a golden glow over the rocks, creating an almost ethereal atmosphere.

Wayne's mind raced with possibilities. Was this "A" connected to the treasure of Padre LaRue? Or was it simply a coincidence, a modern addition to the landscape that had nothing to do with centuries-old Spanish gold?

He knelt down, running his hand over one of the white rocks. It was smooth, worn by years of exposure to the elements. Wayne closed his eyes, trying to imagine what this spot might have looked like hundreds of years ago, when Padre LaRue supposedly roamed these mountains.

"What am I missing here, Padre?" Wayne whispered as his voice carried away by the mountain breeze. "Is this part of your trail, or am I chasing shadows?"

After a few moments of contemplation, Wayne stood up, brushing the dust from his hands. He knew he couldn't linger here too long – the sun was setting, and he still needed to investigate the plane crash site. But something about this "A" nagged at him. It felt significant, even if he couldn't quite put his finger on why.

Wayne prepared to continue along the trail, pulling out his notebook and quickly sketched the "A" and its location. He had a feeling he'd be coming back to this spot, perhaps when he had more pieces of the puzzle to work with.

With one last look at the mysterious landmark, Wayne set off again, his steps purposeful as he followed the path that would lead him to the crash site. The "A" on the mountainside had added yet another layer of intrigue to his hunt, and Wayne couldn't shake the feeling that he was getting closer to unraveling the mystery of the Lost Padre Mine.

The words of Pastor Gonzalez echoed in his mind, reminding him of the stakes involved. This wasn't just about finding treasure – it was about potentially changing lives, about bringing hope to a community struggling against corruption and hardship.

With renewed determination, Wayne pressed on. The crash site awaited, and with it, perhaps, the next clue in this centuries-old treasure hunt. As the last rays of sunlight painted the Franklin Mountains in hues of gold and crimson, Wayne Braddock felt more alive than he had in years, the thrill of the chase coursing through his veins.

Wayne rounded a bend in the trail, suddenly catching sight of something glinting in the distance. Metal, reflecting the late afternoon sun. His heart rate picked up as he quickened his pace.

There, spread across a small plateau, were the remnants of the crashed plane. Time and the elements had taken their toll, but significant pieces of the wreckage remained, a somber monument to a tragedy from decades past.

Wayne approached slowly, his eyes darting from piece to piece of twisted metal. He wasn't sure what he was looking for, but he knew he'd recognize it when he saw it. As he surveyed the crash site, one thought kept running through his mind:

"Alright, Padre LaRue. I'm here. Now show me what you want me to see."

Wayne approached the wreckage cautiously, his eyes scanning every detail. The remnants of the plane were weathered and rusted, barely recognizable as the bomber it once was. He moved carefully among the scattered pieces, his treasure hunter's instincts on high alert for anything out of the ordinary.

Wayne circled the main concentration of wreckage as something caught his eye. Partially buried beneath years of accumulated dirt and plant growth was an object that seemed out of place. Wayne knelt down, brushing away the debris with gloved hands.

What he uncovered made him pause, his brow furrowing in confusion. It was a rusted piece of equipment, but it clearly didn't belong to the plane. As he lifted it from the ground, Wayne realized he was holding an old mine cart sprocket wheel.

"Now what are you doing out here?" he muttered, turning the wheel over in his hands.

The incongruity of finding mining equipment at a plane crash site from the 1950s was not lost on Wayne. This was no coincidence – it was a clue, deliberately left for someone to find. His heart rate quickened as he examined the wheel more closely.

There, barely visible through the rust and corrosion, was a serial number engraved on the metal. Wayne pulled out his notebook, quickly jotting down the number. He knew from experience that such details could be crucial in unraveling complex mysteries.

Wayne stood up, the sprocket wheel heavy in his hands. The presence of this mining artifact at the crash site created a tangible link between the recent past and the centuries-old legend of the Lost Padre Mine. It was as if the layers of history were converging on this very spot.

Wayne glanced around one last time, making sure he hadn't overlooked anything else of significance. The sun was now barely visible above the horizon, painting the sky in brilliant hues of orange and purple. He knew he needed to start making his way back before darkness fell completely.

With a sense of renewed purpose, Wayne began his descent from the crash site, the sprocket wheel tucked securely in his backpack. Each step down the mountain path felt like a step closer to unraveling the mystery that had brought him to El Paso.

Wayne's mind was already working on connecting the dots. The cloth with its kapok fiber, the statue of Fray Garcia de San Francisco, the mysterious "A" on the mountainside, and now this anachronistic piece of mining equipment – all pieces of a puzzle that spanned centuries.

"You may be onto something, Padre Gonzalez," Wayne said aloud, a hint of admiration in his voice. "But I'm starting to see your game."

The lights of El Paso twinkled below, reminding Wayne of the world beyond this treasure hunt. He thought of Pastor Gonzalez and his plea for help, of Selena and her struggles, of a community caught between hope and hardship. The weight of the sprocket wheel in his pack seemed to grow heavier with the responsibility it represented.

Wayne returned to the tramway station, the last vestiges of daylight fading from the sky. He knew that his discovery today was just the beginning. The hunt for the Lost Padre Mine was taking shape, evolving from a vague legend into a tangible mystery with real-world implications.

Boarding the tram for his descent back to the city, Wayne clutched his backpack close, feeling the outline of the sprocket wheel within. Whatever secrets this artifact held, he was determined to uncover them.

~ Chapter 7 ~
The Junkyard

The sun beat down mercilessly on the old Spanish mission, its adobe walls radiating heat even in the cool interior. Padre Gonzalez moved methodically across the earthen floor, his broom stirring up small clouds of dust with each sweep. The young priest's forehead glistened with sweat, whether from the warmth of the day or the weight of his conscience, it wasn't clear.

Gonzalez's eyes kept darting to the corner of the room where an ancient statue stood slightly askew. Its positioning nagged at him, a visual reminder of his recent, clandestine activities within the sacred walls of the mission.

The scrape of the broom against the ground was suddenly interrupted by the creak of a heavy wooden door. Padre Gonzalez's heart leapt into his throat as he saw Padre Oro enter from a side passage. The older missionary moved with the deliberate pace of one who had walked these halls for decades, his weathered face a map of the harsh frontier life.

Gonzalez ceased his sweeping, taking an involuntary step back as Padre Oro approached. He watched nervously, unable to meet the elder priest's eyes. Padre Oro's gaze, however, was fixed on the misplaced statue.

Time seemed to stretch as Padre Oro reached out, his gnarled hands gently grasping the statue. With reverence, he began to reposition it, the scraping of stone against wood echoing in the hushed chamber.

"Padre Gonzalez," Oro's voice broke the silence, the Spanish words heavy with disappointment and a hint of something darker. "¿Qué has hecho?" What have you done?

The simple question carried the weight of accusation, of betrayal, of sins unspoken but known. It was too much for the young priest. The broom slipped from Gonzalez's trembling fingers, clattering to the ground with a sound that seemed to reverberate through the mission like a gunshot.

Gonzalez stood frozen, terror etched across his features. In that moment, as the dust settled around his feet and Padre Oro's piercing gaze bore into him, Padre Gonzalez knew that his secret - whatever it may be - was no longer his alone to bear.

Wayne stood in the cramped hotel room, phone pressed to his ear as he pinned another grainy photograph to the cork board. The image showed the twisted wreckage of a B-36 bomber, its massive frame broken and scattered across a desolate landscape. His eyes darted between the crash site photos and the associated damage reports, mind racing to connect the dots of a decades-old mystery.

Across the room, Selena Martinez sat cross-legged on the couch, her dark hair pulled back in a messy ponytail. Her fingers flew across her smartphone's screen, eyes narrowed in concentration as she scrolled through endless lists of manufacturers. The small metal wheel they had discovered lay next to her, its strange markings catching the light.

Suddenly, Selena's eyes lit up. She punched in a number and held her breath as it rang.

"Yeah, hi," she said, trying to keep the excitement from her voice. After a brief pause, she continued, "Listen, I have this metal wheel, and it has a weird code on it." Another pause. "If I brought it over, do you think you could tell me what it is?"

Wayne glanced over, his eyebrow raised in curiosity. He watched as Selena's face transformed, a grin spreading from ear to ear.

Unable to contain herself, Selena leapt to her feet, phone still clutched to her ear. "I found one!" she exclaimed, bouncing on the balls of her feet.

Wayne dropped the receiver, not bothering to end his own call as he rushed to Selena's side. He peered at her phone screen, heart pounding with anticipation.

Selena ended the call and turned to Wayne, her eyes sparkling with triumph. "Technology One, Stone Age Nothing!!!" she crowed, holding the phone aloft like a trophy.

The pair stood there for a moment, the weight of their potential breakthrough settling over them. The musty hotel room, with its peeling wallpaper and humming air conditioner, suddenly felt like the epicenter of something monumental. They were one step closer to unraveling a mystery that had eluded others for generations.

The sun hung low in the sky, casting long shadows across the dusty landscape as Selena's car rumbled down a deserted road on the outskirts of town. Wayne's knuckles were white on the steering wheel, mind racing with possibilities as he approached his destination.

Ahead, a rusted sign came into view: "Howe's Salvage, Scrap, and Antiquities". Beyond it, piles of twisted metal and discarded machinery stretched as far as the eye could see, a graveyard of forgotten technology and broken dreams.

Wayne eased off the gas, gravel crunching under the tires as he pulled into what passed for a parking lot. He sat for a moment, engine idling, and took in the scene. The junkyard was a maze of towering scrap heaps, old cars stacked precariously atop one another, their paint faded and peeling in the harsh desert sun.

With a deep breath, Wayne cut the engine and stepped out of the car. The air was thick with the scent of rust and oil, punctuated by the occasional screech of metal settling in the heat. He patted his bag, feeling the reassuring shape of the mysterious metal wheel they had discovered.

A weathered wooden door set into a corrugated metal shack. Wayne couldn't shake the feeling that he was being watched. He glanced over his shoulder, but saw only the silent sentinels of junked cars and machinery.

Wayne hesitated for just a moment at the threshold, hand hovering over the tarnished doorknob. Whatever answers lay beyond this door could change everything – not just for him and Selena, but potentially for history itself. With a surge of determination, he grasped the handle and stepped into the unknown depths of the junkyard office.

The door creaked shut behind him, leaving the junkyard in eerie silence. Somewhere in the maze of metal, a crow cawed, as if warning of secrets soon to be unearthed.

Wayne stepped into the dimly lit interior of the junkyard store, a sharp contrast from the bright desert sun momentarily blinded him. The air inside was thick with the scent of old motor oil and musty paperwork. Shelves lined the walls, crammed with an eclectic assortment of car parts, odd machinery, and items Wayne couldn't even begin to identify.

The creak of the floorboards alerted Wayne to another presence. He turned to see the owner shuffling in - an old man dressed in well-worn flannel and overalls, moving with the deliberate pace of someone who had seen too many years of hard labor. The man's limp was pronounced as he made his way behind the cluttered counter.

Wayne saw the elder's nametag, "Howe." He cleared his throat. "Excuse me, Howe, but we called earlier about an odd piece of metal I found in the mountains."

The old man's eyes twinkled with a mix of amusement and suspicion. "Oh yeah? Stealing from the mountains, are we?"

Wayne couldn't help but smile. "No, not really, but yeah, I guess." He pulled out the metal piece, holding it up to catch the light filtering through the dusty windows. "There's a serial number engraved on it. You know what it is?"

Howe took the piece, turning it over in his weathered hands. His voice was gruff but not unkind. "Well, it doesn't look like it would have grown in the mountains. So yes, I think it wouldn't belong there."

"I think it came from a plane crash that happened nearby," Wayne ventured.

Concern flashed across the old man's face. "Plane crash... is everyone alright?"

"Yeah, it was like fifty years ago."

Howe paused, considering the piece once more. "Wait here a moment." He shuffled to a corner of the store, pulling a cloth off what turned out to be a computer screen. Wayne watched, slightly bemused, as the old man began pecking at the keyboard.

"So, you didn't try looking it up on the line?" Howe asked, not taking his eyes off the screen.

Wayne let out a contemptuous breath. "No, I really didn't."

Hold on."

Wayne leaned in, his interest piqued. "Did you find something?"

Abruptly, Howe switched off the screen. "You know what they say... nope!"

"Really?" Wayne couldn't keep the skepticism from his voice.

The old man handed the metal piece back, his expression unreadable. "You know, maybe it's not about this thing, but where that plane was coming and going."

Wayne's mind raced, grasping the implications of the comment. Before he could respond, Howe was holding up a handful of colorful tickets.

"You want some free park tickets?"

Caught off guard, Wayne politely waved them off. "No thanks."

But Howe was insistent, pressing the tickets into Wayne's hands. "Come on, can't beat free!"

Bewildered by the strange turn of events, Wayne accepted the tickets and made his way out of the store. As he stepped back into the harsh sunlight, his mind

72

was reeling. What had the Junkman seen on that screen? And why the sudden change in demeanor?

Inside, unbeknownst to Wayne, Howe returned to his computer. He switched the screen back on, his weathered face illuminated by its glow. With a mixture of contentment and wariness, he glanced towards the door, watching Wayne's retreating figure.

Twenty years in the Air Force hadn't prepared Howe for this – inheriting a treasure trove of history in the heart of El Paso.

He ran his calloused hand over a weathered oak dresser, remembering the day the call came. His father, voice weak and raspy, had finally swallowed his pride and reached out. "Son, I'm not long for this world. The store... it needs you."

Howe had been ready to hang up his wrench for good, dreaming of fishing trips and lazy Sundays. Instead, he found himself surrounded by delicate porcelain, tarnished silver, and the musty smell of aged books, trying to breathe new life into his father's legacy.

As he carefully wound an antique pocket watch, his mind drifted to the precise mechanisms of jet engines and the satisfaction of keeping those magnificent machines airborne. Here, the only things flying were dust motes in the slanted afternoon sunlight.

But there was something about the challenge, about seeing the stories behind each item, that stirred something in Howe. Maybe, just maybe, he could turn this collection of memories into something his old man would've been proud of.

He stood, stretching his aching back, and gazed out at the eclectic array of artifacts from bygone eras. This wasn't the retirement he'd planned, but by God, he'd make it work. After all, whether it was a multimillion-dollar aircraft or a Civil War-era candlestick, everything had a history worth preserving.

~ Chapter 8 ~
Sunland Park

The dim light of the hotel desk lamp cast long shadows across Wayne's room as he sat hunched over his notes. The cork board before him was a chaotic web of photos, newspaper clippings, and scribbled theories, all connected by a maze of red string. His eyes burned from hours of intense focus, but he couldn't shake the feeling that he was on the verge of a breakthrough.

A sharp knock at the door jolted Wayne from his reverie. Before he could fully rise from his chair, the door burst open, and Selena swept into the room like a whirlwind.

"So, I was talking to my boyfriend," she announced without preamble, brushing past Wayne, "and he was saying that too much work can really burn you out."

Wayne pinched the bridge of his nose, feeling a headache coming on. "Selena, I don't have time for this."

But Selena was already examining his board of notes, her keen eyes taking in every detail. "You need to take a breather," she said, her tone softening slightly. "Get out, relax, you know?"

Her gaze fell on the amusement park tickets lying forgotten on the desk. A mischievous grin spread across her face as she snatched them up. "Perfect!"

"Now wait a minute!" Wayne protested, but Selena was already in motion.

She whirled to face him, one finger pointed accusingly. "No, you wait. You remember what happened in Budapest?"

The words hit Wayne like a physical blow. He took an involuntary step back, shoulders slumping as the memory washed over him. The incident in Budapest had been a stark reminder of the dangers of obsession, of pushing too far without pause.

Selena's expression softened, seeing the effect her words had. "You know I'm right," she said, her voice gentler now but no less determined. "We're going to Sunland now!"

Before Wayne could muster another protest, Selena had grabbed his arm and was steering him towards the door. He cast one last, longing look at his board of notes as she pulled him into the hallway.

Wayne felt a mixture of frustration and reluctant gratitude. Part of him knew Selena was right – he had been pushing himself to the brink again. But another part couldn't shake the feeling that the answers he sought were tantalizingly close.

The elevator dinged, and as they stepped inside, Wayne couldn't help but wonder: was this impromptu trip to Sunland a much-needed break, or a dangerous distraction from the truth he was so close to uncovering?

Selena punched the lobby button, her excitement palpable. "Trust me, Wayne," she said, mistaking his thoughtful silence for sulking. "A little fun is exactly what we need right now."

Wayne nodded, forcing a smile. He'd go along with Selena's plan for now. But his mind was already racing, wondering how he could use this unexpected detour to their advantage in their ongoing investigation.

The night air was alive with the distant sounds of laughter and music as Selena's car pulled into the sprawling parking lot of Sunland Amusement Park. Neon lights from the park's entrance cast a kaleidoscope of colors across the windshield, a stark contrast to the somber mood inside the vehicle.

Wayne cut the engine but made no move to exit. His hands remained gripped on the steering wheel, knuckles white with tension. "Selena, this is ridiculous. We should be back at the hotel, working on the case. Every minute we waste here is — "

"Is a minute we're not burning ourselves out," Selena interjected, her tone brooking no argument. She unbuckled her seatbelt and turned to face him fully. "Wayne, I know you. When you get like this, you don't eat, you don't sleep. You just keep pushing until something breaks. And I'm not about to let that happen again."

Wayne's shoulders slumped, the fight draining out of him. "I just feel like we're so close to a breakthrough. That junkyard owner, he knew something. I could see it in his eyes."

Selena's expression softened. She reached out, gently prying one of Wayne's hands from the steering wheel. "And we'll figure it out. But not tonight. Tonight, we're going to eat overpriced cotton candy, ride some roller coasters, and remember what it's like to have fun. Okay?"

For a moment, Wayne said nothing, his gaze fixed on the colorful lights of the park entrance. Finally, he let out a long sigh. "Fine. But just for a couple of hours."

Selena's face lit up with triumph. "That's the spirit! Now come on, I want to see if I can win one of those giant stuffed animals."

Walking across the parking lot, Wayne couldn't help but feel a sense of unease. The case files and theories he'd left behind in the hotel room seemed to call out to him, urging him to return. But as they approached the entrance, the enticing aromas of funnel cakes and popcorn began to work their magic.

They handed their tickets to the attendant, a bored-looking teenager who barely glanced up from his phone. As they passed through the turnstiles, Wayne found himself enveloped by the sights and sounds of the park. Families laughed together, couples walked hand in hand, and the distant screams from roller coaster riders filled the air.

Selena looped her arm through Wayne's, practically bouncing with excitement. "See? Isn't this better than staring at that cork board all night?"

Wayne allowed himself a small smile. "I suppose it beats getting paper cuts from old newspaper clippings."

Venturing deeper into the park, neither of them noticed the dark-clad figure that had been watching them from the shadows of the parking lot. The figure pulled out a cell phone, dialed a number, and spoke in hushed tones before melting back into the darkness.

For better or worse, Wayne and Selena's night of forced fun had begun. But as with all things in their investigation, even a simple trip to an amusement park might hold more surprises than they bargained for.

The evening air was filled with the mingled scents of cotton candy and adrenaline as Wayne and Selena made their way through Sunland Amusement Park. Despite his initial reluctance, Wayne found himself loosening up as they hopped from ride to ride. Selena's laughter was infectious, and he couldn't help but join in as they spun on the teacups and plummeted on the drop tower.

As the night wore on, they found themselves at the foot of the park's crown jewel: The Thunderbolt, a massive roller coaster that loomed against the starry sky. Its steel tracks twisted and curved like a giant serpent, and the screams of its riders echoed across the park.

"Come on, Wayne!" Selena tugged at his arm, practically bouncing with excitement. "We can't leave without riding this!"

Wayne eyed the coaster warily but allowed himself to be pulled into the line. As they inched closer to the loading platform, he felt a mix of anticipation and dread building in his stomach.

Finally, it was their turn. They climbed into the seats, the safety bars clicking into place. Wayne gripped the handlebar tightly, his knuckles white.

Suddenly, a shadow fell over them. A tall, muscular man appeared behind their seats. Before Wayne could react, strong hands gripped his shoulders.

"What the —?" Wayne gasped, twisting in his seat.

The man's voice was deep and menacing, barely above a whisper. "Don't say nothing old man, or the little girl gets it."

Selena, never one to back down, shot back, "Hey! Who are you calling little?"

"Shut up!" the man hissed, his grip on Wayne tightening.

Wayne's mind raced. "What do you want?"

The man leaned in close, his breath hot on Wayne's ear. "We know you're looking for the treasure. Don't!"

The man released Wayne and stepped back. The coaster car jerked forward, beginning its ascent. Wayne twisted in his seat, catching a glimpse of the man making a sign of the cross as he melted into the crowd.

"Wait, stop this, what the hell!" Wayne shouted, but his voice was lost in the mechanical clatter of the coaster.

Cresting the first hill, Wayne's stomach lurched — both from the impending drop and the implications of the man's warning. The car tipped over the edge, and suddenly they were plummeting.

Selena's excited screams filled the air as they hurtled through loops and corkscrews. But Wayne barely noticed the ride's twists and turns. His mind was reeling, trying to process what had just happened. Treasure? What treasure? And who was "we"?

The coaster careened through its final turn as Wayne felt a wave of nausea hit him. Whether from the ride's motion or the sudden complication in their investigation, he couldn't tell.

When the car finally screeched to a halt at the platform, Wayne stumbled out on shaky legs. Selena bounced out behind him, her face flushed with excitement.

"Wasn't that amazing?" she gushed, then paused, noticing Wayne's pale complexion. "Wayne? Are you okay?"

Wayne leaned against a nearby railing, trying to catch his breath. "Selena," he managed to gasp out, "I think our little vacation just got a lot more complicated."

The two made their way towards the exit, Wayne's mind racing. The junkyard owner's cryptic behavior, the mysterious man's warning, talk of treasure — it all swirled in his head like the loops of the roller coaster. One thing was certain: their investigation had taken an unexpected and potentially dangerous turn.

The cacophony of the amusement park seemed to fade into the background as Wayne frantically scanned the crowd, his heart pounding. The mysterious assailant - Pedro, as Wayne had mentally dubbed him - had vanished like a ghost, leaving behind only questions and a lingering sense of unease.

Wayne's eyes darted from face to face, searching for any sign of the muscular thug. But in the sea of excited parkgoers and families, there was no trace of their ominous visitor. It was as if he had never existed at all.

Realizing the futility of his search, Wayne turned back to Selena, concern etched across his features. "Are you alright?" he asked, his voice tight with worry.

Selena, still flushed from the ride and the unexpected confrontation, looked up at Wayne. Her eyes were wide, but not with fear - they sparkled with exhilaration. "That was crazy!!!" she exclaimed, her breath coming in excited gasps.

Wayne let out a long sigh of relief. Leave it to Selena to find thrills in what should have been a terrifying encounter. He shook his head, a mixture of fondness and exasperation washing over him.

Lost in thought, Wayne began to walk away from the roller coaster, his steps slow and deliberate as he tried to make sense of this new development.

"Can we go again?" Selena's eager voice snapped Wayne back to the present. He turned, eyebrows raised in disbelief, to find her grinning from ear to ear, apparently unfazed by the threat they'd just encountered.

"Selena," Wayne began, his tone a mixture of exasperation and admiration, "I think we've had enough excitement for one night. We need to talk about what just happened."

Selena's smile dimmed slightly, but the spark of adventure remained in her eyes. "Oh, come on, Wayne. Where's your sense of adventure? That guy was probably just trying to scare us off. But we're not that easy to intimidate, are we?"

Wayne shook his head, a reluctant smile tugging at the corners of his mouth. "No, we're not. But this changes things, Selena. We need to be careful. That warning... it means we're onto something big."

Wayne's mind was already racing, formulating plans and theories. But Selena's excited chatter about the roller coaster served as a reminder - sometimes, in the midst of danger and mystery, it was important to remember how to have fun.

"Alright," Wayne conceded as they approached the park exit, "we'll come back another time. But right now, we need to get back to the hotel. We've got work to do."

Selena nodded, her expression growing more serious. "You're right. But Wayne?" She paused, a mischievous glint in her eye. "Next time, I'm picking an even bigger roller coaster."

With the night air cool on their faces, Wayne couldn't shake the feeling that they had just taken their first step on a much wilder ride than any amusement park could offer. He also worried more and more how Selena's

85

involvement placed her in increasing danger. Maybe he was not the best person for her to be associated with. Maybe he should just leave altogether, and forget that the treasure even existed. Deep down he knew that once he entered an adventure like this it was difficult to stop altogether. The enticement was too strong to turn his back on, and Wayne hated himself for being this way.

~ Chapter 9 ~
Take the Money and Run

The old tavern was a refuge from the harsh desert sun, its dimly lit interior a stark contrast to the blinding brightness outside. The air was thick with the scent of stale beer and whispered conversations. At the bar, Padre Gonzalez hunched over his glass of scotch, his clerical collar a stark white against the gloom.

Wayne Braddock pushed through the swinging doors, his eyes adjusting to the darkness. He spotted Gonzalez and made his way to the bar, sliding onto the stool next to the priest.

"Bartender, a whiskey, please," Wayne called out. The bartender, a stoic woman with weathered features, nodded silently and reached for a bottle.

Gonzalez stirred, his voice low and slightly slurred. "Any news, Mister Braddock?"

Wayne's jaw tightened. "It would have been fine if it wasn't for all the threats I've been getting. Who the hell else knows what I am doing?"

The priest's eyebrows shot up in surprise. "I don't know what you're talking about."

"I was threatened last night by what I think was a member of some drug cartel!" Wayne hissed, leaning in close.

Gonzalez shook his head emphatically. "Seriously, I don't know anything about that."

Their tense conversation was interrupted by the arrival of Bobby Sue, a young woman in shorts and a t-shirt who seemed out of place in the dingy bar. "Hey tiger, where's the toilet?" she drawled at the bartender, who wordlessly pointed to the side.

As Bobby Sue sauntered off, Wayne turned back to Gonzalez. "I'm not going to be a part of this if it means my life is in danger."

The priest's eyes narrowed. "Calm down, Mr. Braddock. I want you to think about the billions of dollars at stake here."

Wayne fell silent, the weight of those words settling over him like a heavy blanket. Before he could respond,
88

the bar's front door burst open, and a agitated man - Billy Joe - stormed in.

"Bobby Sue, where are you? We gots to go!!!" he bellowed.

Bobby Sue emerged from the restroom, rolling her eyes. "Okay Billy Joe, I heard ya!" She turned to the bartender with a grimace. "You need to clean that toilet!"

The bartender's sarcastic slow clap followed the couple as they hurried out of the bar.

In the sudden quiet, Gonzalez leaned towards Wayne. "So has the cloth helped at all?"

Wayne's mind raced, trying to connect the disparate threads of their investigation. "I have been seeing the kapok symbol at different places, but I haven't tied it all together yet. Speaking of which, I saw this on an old photo from a military plane crash some sixty years ago. You know anything about that?"

Gonzalez's expression turned thoughtful. "Missionaries have been known to help emergencies by being part of the first responders at a major catastrophe. This could have included military operations."

"You think those connections went beyond providing sermons and such?" Wayne pressed.

The priest nodded slowly. "Quite possibly. The church is quite powerful in this region, but so is the military." He paused, his brow furrowing. "There was a crash that was on the Franklin Mountains decades ago. I think it was near one of the high schools... Coronado High, maybe?"

Before Wayne could dig deeper, the bar's door flew open once again. A man in a rumpled suit burst in, brandishing a sheet of paper with mug shots. "Has anyone seen either of these two individuals?" he demanded.

Wayne recognized the mug shots of the couple who had just moments ago been screaming as they ran out of the bar. But he knew that this moment was not a time to be a good Samaritan, as he plenty of his own problems to contend with.

The tavern fell silent, patrons suddenly finding their drinks intensely interesting. The man's face contorted with frustration. "Man, they took the money and run!" he growled, storming back out as quickly as he'd arrived.

In the wake of the detective's departure, Wayne and Gonzalez exchanged meaningful glances. The plot was thickening, with new players entering the game at every turn. As Wayne sipped his whiskey, his mind raced. A sixty-year-old plane crash, a powerful church, military secrets, and now a pair of thieves on the run -

how did it all connect? And more importantly, how deep was he willing to dive to uncover the truth?

The tavern's shadows seemed to deepen around them, as if the very walls were listening to their whispered conspiracy. Wayne couldn't shake the feeling that they were standing on the precipice of something much bigger - and potentially much more dangerous - than they had initially imagined.

The afternoon sun slanted through the dusty hotel room window, casting long shadows across Wayne's makeshift investigation center. The cork board that dominated one wall was a chaotic tapestry of photos, newspaper clippings, and handwritten notes, all interconnected with a web of red string. At its center, a grainy photo of a B-36 bomber's wreckage seemed to stare back at Wayne, challenging him to unravel its secrets.

Wayne stood before the board, the mysterious metal piece from the crash site heavy in his hand. His eyes darted from the piece to the crash photos and back again, his mind racing to connect the dots. Something about the crash had been nagging at him ever since his conversation with Padre Gonzalez in the tavern.

With a determined set to his jaw, Wayne turned to the small table that served as his desk. He spread out a large map of the region, its creases worn from frequent folding and unfolding. Grabbing a ruler and a red marker, he began to work.

Wayne scanned over the flight records he acquired during his research. Referencing the data on hand, his hands moved with practiced precision as he plotted the B-36's last known coordinates and heading. The marker squeaked against the paper as he drew a bold red line, extending the plane's trajectory beyond the crash site.

Wayne's breath caught in his throat as the line continued southward, past the U.S. border and into Mexico. His marker hovered over a point just outside of Juarez, where a small airfield was marked on the map.

"Son of a gun," Wayne muttered, circling the airfield with a decisive stroke of red.

He took a step back, running a hand through his disheveled hair. The implications were staggering. If the B-36 had been heading for this airfield, it meant the crash might not have been an accident at all. But why would a U.S. military aircraft be making a clandestine flight into Mexico?

Wayne's mind raced with possibilities. Smuggling? A covert military operation? Or something even more sinister?

He turned back to the cork board, his eyes landing on the notes about the church's involvement. The padre's words echoed in his mind: "The church is quite powerful in this region, but so is the military."

Wayne grabbed a fresh notecard and scribbled "CHURCH + MILITARY + MEXICO?" in bold letters, pinning it to the board and connecting it to the crash photo with a length of red string.

As he stepped back to survey his work, Wayne couldn't shake the feeling that he was standing on the edge of something massive. The scattered pieces of the puzzle were starting to form a picture, but it was one that grew more dangerous with each new connection.

He glanced at his phone, considering whether to call Selena and share his discovery. But something held him back. The memory of the threat at the amusement park was still fresh, and he couldn't shake the feeling that they were being watched.

No, he decided. He needed more concrete evidence before bringing anyone else into this. Whatever secrets lay hidden in that airfield outside Juarez, Wayne was determined to uncover them – even if it meant crossing the border and putting himself in the crosshairs of forces he was only beginning to understand.

Wayne turned back to the map, his finger tracing the red line to the circled airfield. One thing was certain: his next move would take him into uncharted and potentially perilous territory.

The night was alive with the hum of cicadas and the distant howl of coyotes as Selena's car wound its way along Transmountain Road. The headlights cut through the darkness, illuminating the rugged landscape of the Franklin Mountains. Wayne sat silently, his mind churning with the implications of their journey.

As he rounded a bend, the headlights briefly illuminated a surreal scene: an older Mexican man leading a burro along the roadside. The man turned, his weathered face caught in the glow for just a moment before he and his animal companion melted back into the shadows.

The sight seemed to underscore the complex tapestry of cultures and histories Wayne was delving into with his investigation.

The car continued its descent, leaving the mountains behind as he merged onto Interstate 10. The relative quiet of the mountain road gave way to the steady thrum of highway traffic. Wayne's knuckles were white on the steering wheel, betraying his nervousness about his clandestine mission.

"Are you sure about this, Wayne?" he asked himself, glancing at the oncoming traffic. "Crossing into Mexico... it's not exactly a walk in the park."

Wayne's jaw tightened. As if on cue, he passed under a large green highway sign: "Exit to Juarez, Mexico." The words seemed to hang in the air, a point of no return.

Wayne took a deep breath and flicked on his turn signal. As he veered onto the exit ramp, Wayne couldn't shake the feeling that he was about to cross more than just a geographical border. He was stepping into a world of long-buried secrets and dangerous truths.

The lights of Juarez began to twinkle in the distance, a glittering promise of answers... and potential peril. Wayne's hand instinctively went to his pocket, feeling the reassuring shape of the mysterious metal piece that had started this whole adventure.

"Whatever we find on the other side," Wayne said softly, "we need to be prepared for anything. This goes deeper than we ever imagined."

Wayne kept his eyes fixed on the road ahead. As he approached the border checkpoint, the weight of his mission settled like a heavy blanket. The old B-36 crash, the church's secrets, the military's involvement – it all led here, to this moment.

Wayne's mind raced with possibilities. What would he find at that airfield outside Juarez? And more importantly, who might be waiting for them, determined to keep decades-old secrets buried in the desert sand?

As he joined the line of cars waiting to cross into Mexico, Wayne knew there was no turning back now. Whatever dangers lay ahead, he would face them with the confidence that he would solve a truth that had eluded others for over half a century.

The border loomed before him, a physical manifestation of the threshold he was about to cross – from the familiar into the unknown, from speculation into revelation. As he inched closer to the checkpoint, Wayne couldn't help but wonder: would he find the answers that he sought in Juarez, or would he be stepping into a trap from which there was no escape?

~ Chapter 10 ~
Deserted

The night air was thick with tension as Wayne Braddock approached the airfield in Selena's borrowed car. He killed the headlights as he neared, the poorly lit area ahead barely visible in the dim moonlight. The car's tires crunched softly on the gravel as he pulled up alongside the chain-link fence that encircled the field.

Wayne cut the engine and sat for a moment, his eyes scanning the perimeter. Large, dark shapes of warehouses loomed in the distance, their outlines barely discernible against the night sky. The airfield seemed deserted, but Wayne knew better than to trust appearances.

Taking a deep breath, he opened the car door and stepped out. The cool night air hit his face, carrying with it the faint scent of jet fuel and damp earth. Wayne approached the fence, his fingers wrapping around the cold metal links as he began to climb.

As he reached the top, something caught his eye. A sign, its lettering barely visible in the gloom, hung on the fence. Wayne squinted, making out the Spanish words. A warning sign. He hesitated for a split second, the weight of what he was about to do pressing down on him. But there was no turning back now.

With a grunt of effort, Wayne swung his legs over the top of the fence and dropped down on the other side. He landed in a crouch, his eyes darting left and right, alert for any sign of movement. But the airfield remained still and silent.

Standing up slowly, Wayne brushed off his hands and took stock of his surroundings. He was in. Now came the hard part.

Wayne crept through the airfield, his footsteps muffled by the soft earth beneath his feet. The night seemed to press in around him, broken only by the faint gleam of starlight on metal. Row after row of airplanes stood silent sentinel, their hulking shapes throwing long shadows across the tarmac.

His eyes darted from one aircraft to another, searching. What exactly he was looking for, Wayne wasn't entirely sure. But he knew he'd recognize it when he saw it. His heart pounded in his chest, each beat a reminder of the danger he was in.

Then, suddenly, he saw it. Wayne froze, his gaze locked on a particular plane. Unlike the others, this one bore a distinctive marking - something reminiscent of the Kapok symbol he'd seen before. It was too much of a coincidence to ignore.

Glancing around to ensure he was still alone, Wayne approached the aircraft. He ran his hand along its cool metal surface, feeling the texture of the paint beneath his fingertips. This had to be it.

Taking a deep breath, Wayne grasped the handle of the plane's door. It opened with a soft hiss, and he hoisted himself inside, disappearing into the dark interior. As he settled into the cockpit, surrounded by dials and switches, Wayne couldn't shake the feeling that he'd just crossed a point of no return.

The interior of the plane was pitch black. Wayne fumbled in his pocket for a small flashlight, its beam cutting through the darkness like a knife. He began to search methodically, his hands running over every surface, probing every crevice.

Suddenly, his fingers brushed against something. Wayne's breath caught in his throat as he pulled out a small, metallic object. In the dim light of his flashlight, he could make out the unmistakable shape of a piece from a miner's cart. His heart raced as he turned it over in his palm, feeling its weight. There, etched into the metal, was a serial number - the very same one that matched the sprocket piece he'd found at the crash site.

"I've got it," he whispered to himself, a mix of excitement and dread washing over him.

But his triumph was short-lived. A blinding light suddenly flooded the cabin, causing Wayne to squint and shield his eyes.

"¡Te veo ahí dentro!" a gruff voice called out in Spanish. "¡Sal ahora para que pueda arrestarte!"

Wayne's blood ran cold. He'd been discovered. Instinctively, he ducked down, trying to avoid the beam of light sweeping across the interior. His mind raced, searching for a way out of this predicament.

The sound of heavy boots on metal told Wayne the guard was climbing into the plane. Panic surged through him as the beam of light found him, pinning him in place like a butterfly to a board. The metallic click of a gun being cocked echoed in the confined space.

In that moment, Wayne made a desperate decision. He lunged forward, attempting to rush past the guard and make a break for it. But he'd underestimated his opponent.

A meaty hand grabbed him, fingers digging into his flesh with bruising force. Wayne struggled, but it was futile. The last thing he felt was a sharp pain exploding in his head, and then the world went black. Wayne slumped unconscious to the floor of the plane.

Consciousness returned to Wayne slowly, like waves lapping at a distant shore. The first thing he became aware of was pain — a dull, throbbing ache that seemed to envelope his entire skull. The second was heat — an oppressive, all-consuming heat that pressed down on him from all sides.

Wayne's eyes fluttered open, immediately squinting against the harsh glare of sunlight. For a moment, he lay still, trying to make sense of his surroundings. The ground beneath him was hard and gritty. Sand. He was lying on sand.

With a groan, Wayne pushed himself up to a sitting position, his head spinning from the effort. As his vision cleared, the full reality of his situation came into focus. Desert stretched out in every direction, an endless sea of sand and rock. In the far distance, he could make out the hazy outlines of mountain ridges, shimmering in the heat like a mirage.

The sun hung high in a cloudless sky, beating down mercilessly. Wayne raised a hand to shield his eyes, scanning the horizon for any sign of civilization. There was nothing. No roads, no buildings, not even a cactus. Just the vast, empty expanse of the desert.

Panic began to rise in Wayne's chest, but he forced it down. He needed to think clearly if he was going to survive this. Instinctively, his hand went to his pocket, searching for... something. His fingers brushed against cool metal, and a smile of relief crossed his parched lips. The miner's cart piece was still there. Whatever else had happened, at least he hadn't lost that.

Wayne struggled to his feet, his body protesting every movement. He wiped his forearm across his brow, already slick with sweat. The heat was oppressive, seeming to suck the moisture from his body with every breath.

For a moment, Wayne stood still, considering his options. He thought that the only direction which might lead to safety would be north, as America was north of Mexico. With one last look at the sun, which was descending downward to his left, Wayne chose a forward direction and started walking. Each step was an effort, his feet sinking slightly into the loose sand.

The sun had begun its descent towards the horizon when Wayne first caught sight of the building. At first, he thought it must be a mirage, another cruel trick of the desert. But as he drew closer, stumbling on legs weak from exhaustion and dehydration, the structure solidified into reality.

It was a bar, or what remained of one. The building looked like it had been plucked straight out of an old Western film and left to rot in the unforgiving desert. Its weathered wooden exterior was bleached gray by countless days under the punishing sun. A crooked sign, its letters long since faded beyond recognition, creaked softly in the hot breeze.

Wayne paused, blinking in disbelief. His appearance had changed dramatically since his ordeal began. His once-crisp clothes now hung from his frame in tattered, filthy rags. A scraggly beard had begun to sprout on his chin, and his skin was reddened and peeling from sun exposure. He looked every bit the desert wanderer he had become.

For a long moment, Wayne simply stood there, swaying slightly on his feet. The sight of the bar, as decrepit as it was, filled him with a profound sense of relief. It was the first sign of human habitation he'd seen in what felt like an eternity.

There was no logical reason for anyone to frequent such an establishment, let alone operate it. The very existence of the bar in this desolate landscape defied reason. And yet, here it stood.

Wayne licked his cracked lips, his parched throat aching at the mere thought of a drink. Whether the place was open or long abandoned, it at least offered the promise of shade. And maybe, just maybe, there might be water inside.

With renewed determination, Wayne forced his leaden feet to move. Each step was an effort, but the bar's ramshackle porch was a beacon drawing him forward. As he approached the weather-beaten door, a mix of hope and apprehension filled his chest.

What would he find inside? Help? Danger? Or just more emptiness?

There was only one way to find out. Wayne reached for the door handle, the warm metal rough against his blistered palm. Whatever awaited him beyond this threshold, he knew it would be the next chapter in his increasingly bizarre adventure.

Wayne stumbled through the door, the dim interior of the bar a stark contrast to the blinding desert sun. The cool air washed over him, bringing momentary relief. He blinked, his eyes slowly adjusting to the gloom.

The bar was sparsely populated, a few rough-looking patrons nursing drinks in the corners. Wayne made his way to the counter, his parched throat driving him forward.

"Can I get some water please?" he croaked, his voice barely above a whisper.

The waitress behind the counter turned, her eyes narrowing as she took in Wayne's disheveled appearance. Her lips curled in disgust.

"We don't serve the homeless," she snapped. "Take your business elsewhere."

Wayne's heart sank. "You don't understand..." he began, desperately.

The waitress cut him off. "Oh, I understand," she said, her voice dripping with contempt. "Wally!"

From behind the kitchen, a mountain of a man emerged. The cook, presumably Wally, lumbered towards Wayne, meaty hands outstretched.

Before Wayne could react, Wally grabbed him by the shirt. There was a loud rip as the already tattered fabric gave way, exposing Wayne's sun-blistered skin.

Just as Wayne braced himself for the worst, a voice cut through the tension.

"That's enough."

The words were quiet but carried an unmistakable air of authority. Wayne turned to see a man had risen from one of the tables. He was lean and weathered, with eyes that seemed to see right through you.

Wally hesitated, his grip on Wayne loosening. The newcomer stared him down, not saying another word. After a tense moment, Wally backed away, retreating to the kitchen.

The man turned his penetrating gaze to Wayne. "You're Wayne Braddock," he stated. It wasn't a question.

Despite his dire situation, Wayne couldn't help but smile. He brushed off the remnants of his shirt. "Yes, yes I am." Relief washed over Wayne. Finally, a stroke of luck.

"Great," he said, his stomach growling audibly. "Let's get some food." The man's lips twitched in what might have been amusement. "And possibly a new shirt," he added, eyeing Wayne's exposed torso.

As they moved towards a table, Wayne studied his unexpected savior. "I'm grateful for your help, but... who are you?"

The man met Wayne's gaze. "My name is Kitto," he said simply. "And I believe we have much to discuss, Mr. Braddock."

~Chapter 11~

Johnny Kitto

The highway stretched out before them, a ribbon of asphalt cutting through the desert landscape. With Wayne riding behind him, Johnny Kitto's dark motorcycle roared beneath them, eating up the miles with a steady rhythm. Wayne clung to his newfound ally, the wind whipping at his ridiculous UFO t-shirt — a temporary replacement for his tattered rags.

Kitto loved the feel of the highway, the thunderous purr of his Indian motorcycle drowning out everything but the wild beating of his heart. His hair whipped behind him, a banner of defiance against the world that had never quite known what to make of him. Half

Spanish, half Native American, Johnny had always straddled two worlds, never fully belonging to either. But out here on the open road, none of that mattered. He was free, untethered, the master of his own destiny. The intricate tattoos adorning his arms told the story of his people – the Mescalero Apache – their triumphs, their struggles, their enduring spirit. Johnny wore them like armor, a reminder of who he was and where he came from.

Those who knew him spoke of his generosity, his unwavering loyalty to those who earned his respect. He'd given a helping hand to more stranded motorists than he could count, shared his last dollar with fellow riders down on their luck. But cross him or disrespect his tribal nation, and you'd find yourself facing a man as unyielding as the ancient mesas of his ancestral lands. Johnny lived by his own code – one of honor, freedom, and an unshakeable connection to the land and its people. The road stretched endlessly before him, full of promise and adventure. He was exactly where he belonged – on the edge of everywhere, ready for whatever lay around the next bend.

Wayne's mind raced with questions. Finally, he raised his voice over the engine's rumble. "Why did you help me?"

Kitto's response was measured, his words carried back to Wayne on the wind. "You helped the Cherokee Nation retrieve ancient burial jewels. I remember this."

The memory flashed through Wayne's mind — another adventure, another time. "Yeah, I did do that," he confirmed, surprised. "Are you Cherokee?"

"Yeah," Kitto replied simply. After a pause, he added, "Today is your lucky day, my friend."

Wayne couldn't help but chuckle. "Ordained by the eagle spirit?" he joked, referencing a bit of Cherokee lore he'd picked up during that past adventure.

Kitto's reply was dry. "I wouldn't go that far."

As the landscape blurred past them, Wayne's curiosity got the better of him. "Where was I?" he asked, trying to piece together the gaps in his memory.

"Outside of Socorro, Texas," Kitto answered.

Wayne blinked in surprise. "Really? With this shirt, I would have guessed Roswell, New Mexico." He plucked at the gaudy UFO design adorning his chest.

A low chuckle rumbled from Kitto. "No, that shirt just makes me laugh."

Wayne grinned, appreciating the unexpected humor from his stoic companion. As they continued down the highway, he felt a mix of relief and anticipation. He was out of immediate danger, thanks to Kitto, but he knew his journey was far from over. Wayne's grin then became serious again, as he began calculating how difficult it would be to transport him from Mexico back into the United States. He couldn't figure out how he crossed the border, but at least he knew that he was thankful for not being stranded in the desert anymore.

The desert stretched endlessly around them, a stark reminder of the ordeal Wayne had just survived. Yet, as the wind rushed past and the motorcycle carried them towards an unknown destination, Wayne felt a spark of hope. Whatever challenges lay ahead, he was no longer facing them alone. He tightened his grip on Kitto's jacket, his mind turning to the piece of the miner's cart still tucked safely in his pocket. There were still mysteries to solve, dangers to face. But for now, Wayne was content to let the open road carry him forward, one mile at a time.

The sun was high in the sky as Kitto's motorcycle rumbled into Wayne's hotel parking lot. Selena, who had been sitting on the curb, her face etched with worry, jumped to her feet as she recognized Wayne. Wayne dismounted, still wearing the ridiculous UFO t-shirt. Selena rushed towards him, her eyes wide with shock and relief.

110

"Oh my god, what happened to you?" she exclaimed, taking in his disheveled appearance and the strange shirt.

Wayne ran a hand through his unkempt hair, feeling the weight of his recent ordeal. "It's a long story," he said, his voice carrying a mix of exhaustion and resignation.

Selena's gaze shifted to Kitto, who remained astride the motorcycle, his stoic presence a stark contrast to Wayne's bedraggled state. "And who is this guy?" she asked, suspicion creeping into her voice.

Wayne started walking past Selena towards the hotel entrance, fatigue evident in every step. "His name is Kitto," he called over his shoulder.

"Johnny Kitto," the man on the motorcycle clarified, his voice calm and steady.

Selena's brow furrowed as she processed this bizarre situation. Suddenly, a thought struck her. "Where is my car?" she demanded, her tone sharp with sudden worry.

Wayne froze mid-step, his back to Selena. His eyes darted left and right as he searched for an answer, his mind racing through the events that had led him here. After a moment, he let out a heavy sigh. Turning on his heel, Wayne walked back to the motorcycle. "Come on, we're going to Mexico," he announced, his voice filled with a mixture of determination and resignation.

"Mexico?" Selena echoed, disbelief coloring her voice.

Kitto, who had been silently observing the exchange, finally spoke up. "Okay," he said, his tone neutral. Then, eyeing Wayne's grimy state, he added, "But maybe after you shower?"

Wayne looked back at Kitto, then down at himself. He gave a reluctant nod, acknowledging the wisdom in the suggestion. Without another word, he turned and headed inside the hotel, leaving Selena standing in the parking lot, her expression a mix of confusion and growing concern.

Selena turned to Kitto, her eyes demanding answers. But the enigmatic man simply sat on his motorcycle, his face unreadable. The desert wind whistled through the parking lot, carrying with it the promise of more adventures — and more complications — to come.

Now back in Mexico, the motorcycle's engine growled to a stop as Wayne and Kitto arrived at the airfield. Wayne dismounted, his eyes scanning the familiar landscape. But something was terribly wrong. Where there had once been hangars, planes, and bustling activity, there was now... nothing. Only a dusty airstrip and Selena's car remained, stretching out before him like a ghostly reminder of what had been.

Wayne turned to Kitto, a mix of gratitude and determination in his eyes. "Kitto, thank you for everything. I can take it from here."

Kitto's stoic expression flickered with concern. "Are you sure, boss?"

Wayne nodded, his jaw set. "Yeah, you've helped enough. Thanks."

With a rev of his engine, Kitto rode off, leaving Wayne alone in the eerie emptiness of the airfield. Wayne smiled as he though how he was eternally thankful to the random yet life-saving friendship he had just made.

Kneeling down, Wayne ran his hand over the tarmac, feeling the rough texture beneath his fingers. Confusion etched deep lines in his forehead as he surveyed the barren landscape. His gaze fell on a crumpled warning sign lying on the ground, its Spanish text a mocking reminder of his previous misadventure. Wayne Braddock stood at the edge of the vast expanse, his eyes scanning the shimmering horizon where heat waves danced above the desert floor. The airfield stretched before him, a stark testament to human ambition amid nature's desolation. His mind, ever calculating, began to dissect the monumental task at hand. How much would it take to make this place vanish without a trace?

He ran through the numbers in his head, each figure a piece in a complex puzzle. The runway alone – nearly two miles of reinforced concrete – would require an army of workers and a fleet of heavy machinery to break up and haul away. Then there were the hangars, control tower, and various outbuildings. Wayne's fingers twitched, itching for a notepad. He estimated it would take at least 200 men working round the clock for weeks, maybe months. Heavy equipment operators, demolition experts, truckers to transport the debris – and that was just for the visible structures.

And then there was the matter of secrecy. How do you move an entire airfield without drawing attention? It would require a cover story, carefully orchestrated supply lines, and enough money to keep everyone involved silent. Wayne allowed himself a grim smile. It was an impossible task for most, but he'd bet there were nefarious individuals that could achieve the impossible, even if illegally. With the right resources, the right team, and enough determination, he could make this airfield disappear like a mirage in the desert heat.

Or was the airfield even real? Maybe what Wayne had visited earlier was a facade, a temporary construct that was placed to deter Wayne from finding the real truth? So many possibilities raced through his mind, and Wayne didn't know which scenario to believe. The question now was: who wanted it gone badly enough to pay the price?

Selena's car, still parked where he had left it what felt like a lifetime ago. It was an incongruous sight in the otherwise deserted airfield. He approached Selena's car, his mind racing with possibilities and questions.

Suddenly, the roar of an engine shattered the silence. Wayne whirled around to see another vehicle speeding towards him, kicking up a cloud of dust in its wake. Before he could react, the car screeched to a halt, and two armed men leapt out.

"¿No aprendiste la primera vez?" one of them growled in Spanish as they grabbed Wayne, roughly shoving him towards their car.

Wayne struggled, but it was futile. The men, whom he would later learn were called Manuel and Pedro, were too strong and too determined. In a matter of moments, he found himself thrust into the backseat of their vehicle. As they peeled away, Wayne caught a glimpse of Pedro jumping into Selena's car. The two vehicles sped off, leaving behind nothing but swirling dust and unanswered questions.

Wayne's heart raced as he tried to make sense of what was happening. The empty airfield, the sudden appearance of these men, the cryptic Spanish taunt - it all pointed to a deeper, more dangerous game than he had imagined. As the landscape blurred past the car window, Wayne realized that his adventure had just taken a far more perilous turn. Then they placed a blindfold over his head.

~Chapter 12~
Do Not Cross the Cartel

The sun beat down mercilessly as the two-car convoy wound its way through the desert landscape. Wayne, still reeling from the sudden turn of events. Wayne tried to make sense of where they were headed.

Ahead of them, Pedro navigated Selena's car with practiced ease. Wayne felt a pang of guilt thinking about Selena and how he'd have to explain the fate of her vehicle - assuming he got the chance.

As they crested a hill, a structure came into view. Rising from the barren landscape like a mirage was a sprawling mansion, its white walls gleaming in the harsh sunlight. It was a jarring sight, this opulent dwelling surrounded by nothing but sand and scrub brush for miles.

The cars slowed as they approached an ornate gate. Lush greenery lined the driveway, a testament to the wealth and power required to maintain such an oasis in this unforgiving environment.

The vehicles pulled up to the front of the mansion. Wayne's mind raced. Who lived here? What did they want with him? And how did all of this connect to the vanished airfield and the mysterious artifact he'd found?

Manuel brought the car to a stop, the crunch of gravel under the tires seeming unnaturally loud in the eerie quiet. Wayne's hands clenched involuntarily as they removed his blindfold, his body tense with anticipation and fear.

Pedro parked Selena's car alongside them, Wayne catching his reflection in the window. His face was etched with worry and exhaustion. He took a deep breath, steeling himself for whatever came next.

The car door opened, and Manuel's gruff voice broke the silence. "Out," he commanded.

Wayne stepped out into the blazing sun, squinting as he took in the full grandeur of the mansion before him. Whatever answers he sought, he had a feeling he was about to find them - for better or worse.

Wayne was led towards the imposing front doors. He couldn't shake the feeling that he was walking into the lion's den. But there was no turning back now. His adventure had brought him here, and here he would face whatever awaited him.

The opulence of the mansion's interior gave way to the dazzling sunlight of the poolside area. Wayne squinted as Manuel roughly guided him through the patio doors. The expansive pool stretched before them, its azure waters a stark contrast to the arid landscape beyond.

At the far end of the pool stood a man, his back to them. Even from behind, his well-tailored suit and confident posture exuded authority.

"Siéntate, gringo," Manuel growled, shoving Wayne into a nearby chair. Wayne grunted as he landed, his eyes darting around, taking in his surroundings before settling on the man by the pool.

As if on cue, the man turned, his dark features breaking into a wide smile. He spread his arms in a welcoming gesture, the ice in his drink clinking softly.

"Ah, my American friend," he said, his voice smooth and cultured. "Welcome to my lovely home. I hope the ride was not too uncomfortable."

Wayne's lips twisted into a sardonic smile. "Of course not," he retorted, "it was everything I hoped for from the cartel."

The man's eyebrows shot up in feigned surprise. "Cartel? Is that what you think of me?" He gestured at his surroundings. "What, because I dress well, live in the desert in this magnificent mansion, I must be a drug dealer?"

Wayne felt a twinge of discomfort, suddenly aware of how his words might have sounded. He grimaced, looking down at his feet.

The man strode towards him, his voice taking on an edge. "That, my American friend, is what we like to call racism!" He turned to Manuel, switching to rapid-fire Spanish. "Manuel, ¿trajiste a un racista a mi casa?"

Manuel shrugged, shaking his head.

Turning back to Wayne, the man's tone softened slightly. "My associate says you do not seem to be a racist. Maybe you have a personal problem with me. Is this what this is about, Mr. Braddock?"

Wayne's head snapped up at the use of his name. "I am not a racist," he said firmly. "I am, however, not one accustomed to being kidnapped!"

The man's smile returned, though it didn't reach his eyes. "Well, I'm sorry, but you left me no choice. You see, I take exception to nosy people that come to my secret airstrip."

Wayne leaned forward, keeping his voice low. "I suspect that it was not really yours to begin with."

There was a pause as the man regarded Wayne with newfound interest. "So, who do you think the airstrip belonged to then?"

"If I were a betting man, I'd say your government."

The man's smile widened. He turned to his thugs, speaking in Spanish. "¡Este es un americano inteligente!" Then, leaning in close to Wayne, his voice dropped to a menacing whisper. "I don't like smart Gringos."

Just as quickly, he straightened, his demeanor shifting once more to affable host. "But he is right, you know. Back in the day, I don't know, maybe the 1940s or so, the United States and Mexico had some sort of secret military thing going on. Then, it suddenly stopped. No more flights. So, my grandfather, he took the airstrip, and we have been using it ever since for... international relations."

Wayne met the man's gaze unflinchingly. "You mean drugs."

The tension around the pool ratcheted up several notches. Wayne could feel Manuel tensing behind him, ready to act at a moment's notice. But as he stared into the dark eyes of his captor, Wayne knew he was stepping into dangerous territory. Yet, he couldn't back down now. Too much was at stake, and somewhere in this web of lies and half-truths lay the answers he sought.

The man who Wayne now assumed must be Trujillo, regarded him with a mixture of amusement and irritation. The next few moments, Wayne realized, could determine whether he walked out of here alive or not.

Trujillo's smile turned predatory as he pointed at Wayne, then turned to Pedro. "Tráela," he commanded in Spanish.

Wayne watched warily as Pedro left the pool area, his mind racing to understand what was happening.

Trujillo's attention returned to Wayne. "Your surprise visits have impacted my business affairs," he said, his tone casual but with an underlying threat. "You and your search for gold has brought you to my nice little airstrip."

Wayne's surprise must have shown on his face because Trujillo's smile widened. "There is no such thing as the lost Spanish gold," he continued. "That myth about Padre LaRue is a hoax, to keep people distracted from what is really going down. You get treasure hunters searching all over the Franklin Mountains, in Juarez, everywhere, and nothing is ever found."

Before Wayne could process this information, movement caught his eye. Pedro had returned, roughly pushing a familiar figure into the pool area.

"Wayne?" Selena's voice was filled with confusion and fear.

Wayne tried to stand, but Manuel's iron grip forced him back down. He could only watch helplessly as Selena was seated across from him.

Trujillo's hand moved to the small of his back, pulling out a gun. The sight of the weapon sent a chill down Wayne's spine.

"Mr. Braddock," Trujillo said, his voice low and dangerous, "I want you to hear me one time with this." He walked towards Selena, the gun glinting in the sunlight. "I want you to never come to my airstrip, or to my mansion, or anywhere near my immediate vicinity again."

Wayne's heart pounded as Trujillo pressed the gun to Selena's temple. "And you should give up any notion of Spanish gold."

"Please, don't hurt her!" Wayne pleaded, his voice cracking with desperation.

Trujillo's eyebrow arched. "Why, because she is your daughter?"

Wayne's head whipped between Trujillo and Selena, shock evident on his face. How could Trujillo know this? He hadn't even told Selena yet.

"Daughter?" Selena echoed, her eyes wide with disbelief.

"Do we understand each other?" Trujillo's voice cut through the tension like a knife.

Wayne felt the fight drain out of him. He turned his face away, shame and regret washing over him. "Yes," he muttered.

Trujillo's demeanor instantly changed. He lowered the gun, his face breaking into a wide smile. "Excellent! I told you, this is one smart gringo!" He paused, then waved his hand dismissively. "Okay, you can leave now!"

Wayne and Selena rose shakily to their feet. As Manuel and Pedro escorted them out of the mansion, Wayne's mind was a whirlwind of emotions and questions. The myth of the Spanish gold debunked, his secret revealed, and now this ominous warning – it was all too much to process.

Stepping outside the mansion, Wayne knew that while one chapter of their adventure had closed, another, far more complex one was just beginning. He glanced at Selena, seeing the hurt and confusion in her eyes. There would be a lot to explain, and he wasn't sure where to start. The gates of the mansion clanged shut behind them, a final reminder of the dangerous world they'd just escaped.

Trujillo leaned back in his leather chair, fingers steepled beneath his chin. The opulent office of his hacienda offered little comfort as his mind raced, fixated on one man: Wayne Braddock.

The American was becoming a thorn in his side, sniffing too close to secrets buried for centuries. Trujillo poured himself a glass of añejo tequila, savoring the burn as he contemplated his options. He thought that Braddock wasn't some low-level smuggler or rival gangster. The man had connections, resources, and was well known. His disappearance would raise too many questions.

"Dios mío," Trujillo muttered, rubbing his temples. "Why can't he just let sleeping dogs lie?"

The gold was more than mere wealth; it was history, power, legitimacy. In the right hands – his hands – it could reshape the balance of power in the region. But in Braddock's? It would be nothing more than a historical footnote, a museum piece.

He reached for his phone, a grim smile playing on his lips. Trujillo felt confident that Wayne Braddock's search for the mission gold had come to an end.

~Chapter 13 ~

Wayne Meets His Daughter

The desert stretched endlessly before them, a sea of sand and scrub brush undulating beneath the merciless sun. Inside Selena's car, the tension was palpable, thick enough to cut with a knife. Wayne's hands gripped the steering wheel tightly, his knuckles white with strain. Selena sat rigidly in the passenger seat as her gaze fixed on the barren landscape rushing past.

Wayne cleared his throat, breaking the heavy silence. "Selena..." he began, his voice tentative.

"Don't say anything to me," Selena snapped, cutting him off before he could continue. Her words hung in the air, sharp and final.

Wayne's mouth closed with an audible click. He turned his attention back to the road, his shoulders slumping slightly. The silence stretched on, broken only by the hum of tires on asphalt and the car's laboring air conditioning.

Suddenly, Selena whirled to face him, her eyes blazing with a mixture of hurt and anger. "You're my father?!" The words exploded from her, a dam of emotion finally breaking.

Wayne sighed heavily, his grip on the steering wheel tightening even further. "Yes," he admitted softly, the single word carrying the weight of years of secrets and regrets.

"And you never thought to tell me about this?" Selena's voice trembled with barely contained fury.

Wayne's eyes flicked briefly to her before returning to the road. "Your mother and I had an agreement," he said, the words sounding hollow even to his own ears.

Selena's face contorted with disgust. "¡Eso es tan típico de un hombre que no acepta la responsabilidad!" she spat in rapid Spanish. Then, switching back to English, she continued, "Don't blame Mom for what you decided NOT to do!"

She turned away from him, her profile rigid with anger as she stared out the passenger window.

"I wanted to tell you..." Wayne started, his voice pleading.

But Selena cut him off again, her words like ice. "I said don't say anything to me."

The car fell silent once more, the weight of unspoken words and years of absence hanging heavily between them. Wayne's mind raced, trying to find the right words to bridge the chasm that had suddenly opened between them. But he knew that right now, any attempt at explanation would only widen the gap.

Continuing down the dusty highway, Wayne couldn't help but feel that this revelation had changed everything. The adventure that had brought them together now threatened to tear them apart. And as the miles rolled by beneath their wheels, he wondered if there was any way to repair the damage that had been done.

The desert stretched on, indifferent to their personal drama. But for Wayne and Selena, the landscape of their relationship had shifted irrevocably, and neither was sure what lay on the horizon.

The sun was beginning to dip towards the horizon as Wayne guided Selena's car into the driveway of her modest home. The tension that had built during their journey hung heavy in the air, an almost tangible presence between them.

Before Wayne could even put the car in park, Selena was moving. She flung open the passenger door, her movements sharp with anger. In one fluid motion, she exited the vehicle, slamming the door behind her with a force that made the entire car shake. The sound echoed in the quiet neighborhood, a physical manifestation of her fury.

Wayne winced at the noise, then quickly leaned across the front seat, his hand fumbling to roll down the passenger window. "Selena," he called out, his voice tinged with desperation, "I... I still need to use the car."

Selena didn't break her stride or turn to face him. Her back was ramrod straight, shoulders tense as she marched towards her front door. Her voice, when it came, was cold and biting. "Do whatever you want, Dad."

The word 'Dad' was loaded with sarcasm and hurt, striking Wayne like a physical blow. He watched helplessly as Selena disappeared into her house, the front door closing firmly behind her.

For a long moment, Wayne sat there, his hands gripping the steering wheel, staring at the closed door. The weight of years of absence, of secrets kept and truths withheld, seemed to press down on him. He wanted to go after her, to explain, to make things right. But he knew that right now, any attempt at reconciliation would only be met with more anger.

With a heavy sigh, Wayne put the car in reverse. As he backed out of the driveway, his eyes lingered on Selena's home, on the life he'd been absent from for so long. The adventure that had brought them together now seemed to have driven an even deeper wedge between them.

As he drove away, the setting sun casting long shadows across the road, Wayne couldn't shake the feeling that he'd lost something precious, something he hadn't even known he had until it was too late. The road ahead seemed uncertain, filled with challenges both physical and emotional.

But as the house receded in his rearview mirror, Wayne steeled his resolve. He had a mystery to solve, a danger to face. And maybe, just maybe, in the process of unraveling the secrets of the lost Spanish gold, he could find a way to mend the broken bonds with his daughter.

The car disappeared around a corner, leaving behind a quiet street and a house filled with unresolved emotions, as the day's last light painted the sky in hues of orange and pink.

Wayne guided Selena's car into the dusty lot of the junkyard. The familiar landscape of rusted metal and discarded machinery stretched out before him, but something was off. The usual bustle of activity was

131

absent, replaced by an eerie stillness that sent a chill down Wayne's spine despite the heat.

He pulled into the empty parking lot, the crunch of gravel under the tires seeming unnaturally loud in the silence. As he cut the engine, Wayne's eyes swept across the deserted yard. No other vehicles were in sight, not even the battered pickup truck the old junkman usually kept parked by the office.

With a sense of unease growing in his gut, Wayne stepped out of the car. The hot air hit him like a wall, carrying the acrid scent of hot metal and old oil. His footsteps echoed as he approached the weathered wooden building that served as the junkyard's office.

Nearing the door, something caught Wayne's eye. A piece of paper was tacked to the weathered wood, fluttering slightly in the hot breeze. Next to it hung a simple "CLOSED" sign, its finality striking Wayne like a physical blow.

He leaned in closer, his heart sinking as he recognized the somber black border of a newspaper obituary. The junkman's wrinkled face stared back at him from a grainy photograph, below which was printed the stark announcement of his recent passing.

Wayne stood frozen, the shock of the unexpected news washing over him. Now, he was gone, taking with him whatever knowledge he might have had about Wayne's current mystery.

For a long moment, Wayne stayed there, his hand resting on the sun-warmed wood of the door frame. The loss of the junkman was not just a personal blow, but a potential setback in his quest. Who else might have the kind of obscure knowledge the old man had possessed?

With a heavy sigh, Wayne turned away from the door. There was nothing more to be done here. As he walked back to the car, his footsteps seemed to echo with a newfound sense of urgency. Time was passing, people were leaving, and the answers he sought seemed to be slipping further from his grasp.

Sliding back behind the wheel, Wayne's mind was already racing, trying to figure out his next move. The adventure was taking unexpected turns, and he couldn't shake the feeling that the stakes were getting higher with each passing day.

With one last glance at the silent junkyard, Wayne started the engine and pulled away. The quest for the lost Spanish gold – if it even existed – had just become more complicated. But Wayne Braddock was not one to back down from a challenge, no matter how daunting it might seem.

As Selena's car disappeared down the dusty road, the junkyard stood silent under the blazing sun, its secrets now forever locked away with its departed caretaker.

A buzz on Wayne's antiquated cell phone triggered. Pulling it out of his pocket while still driving, Wayne caught that he had a new text message. Thumbing through the buttons, he read the message as a sense of dread began to sneak up on him.

Come to dinner. Fix this with Selena.

"Dinner with Maria," Wayne thought. This can't be good.

~ Chapter 14 ~

Longest Dinner Ever

The night was quiet in the Martinez household, save for the sudden rapping at the front door. Maria, Selena's mother, padded down the hallway, her feet whispering against the hardwood floor. She opened the door, revealing Wayne Braddock standing on the porch, his face a mask of apprehension.

"What the hell were you thinking telling Selena?" Maria hissed, her voice barely above a whisper. Her eyes darted back towards the depths of the house, wary of being overheard.

Wayne raised his hands in a placating gesture, his shoulders hunched as if to make himself smaller. "It

135

wasn't my choice!" he protested, his voice matching Maria's hushed tones.

Maria's lips pressed into a thin line, her frustration palpable. "I've been on damage control ever since she got back!" She ran a hand through her hair, disheveled from hours of worry.

"I'm sorry, really!" Wayne's apology seemed genuine, but it did little to soften Maria's expression.

She sighed, her anger deflating slightly. "I only invited you over to fix things with her."

Wayne nodded, understanding the gravity of the situation. "Okay," he said simply, knowing that actions would speak louder than words at this point.

Maria stepped aside, gesturing for Wayne to enter. As he crossed the threshold, she closed the door behind him with a soft click, sealing them both in the tense atmosphere of the house. The hallway stretched before them, leading to whatever confrontation awaited with Selena.

The dining room was thick with tension as Selena, Maria, and Wayne sat around the table, their plates barely touched. The clink of silverware against china seemed unnaturally loud in the strained silence. Finally, Selena's voice cut through the awkwardness.

"Okay, so now I know. Wayne is my Dad. I got it. Why didn't anyone at least tell me?" Her words hung in the air, demanding an answer.

Wayne and Maria exchanged a look, their silence speaking volumes. Selena pressed on, her frustration evident. "I'm an adult now. I'm like nineteen! I could handle this, you know."

Maria turned to her daughter, regret etched on her face. "You're absolutely right, sweetheart. I should have told you a long time ago."

Wayne, seemingly uncomfortable, offered weakly, "Maybe it was better off that you not know?"

"What?" Selena's incredulity was palpable.

Maria shot Wayne a withering glare. "He's not being serious, are you?"

Wayne backpedaled quickly. "No, of course not. We should have told you a long time ago, Selena."

"So what are you going to do about the treasure?" Selena asked, turning to her father, Wayne. Her voice held a mixture of excitement and hope that made her mother, Maria, wince.

Maria's eyes narrowed as she looked between her daughter and her husband. "Is this what this was all about? A treasure hunt?" The disbelief in her voice was palpable, tinged with a weariness that spoke of too many schemes and too many disappointments.

Wayne shifted uncomfortably under his wife's scrutiny. "Come on, Maria. You're talking about my livelihood," he said, his voice a blend of defensiveness and pleading. The lines on his face seemed to deepen as he spoke, telling the story of a man who had chased one too many dreams.

"You don't need to be getting Selena involved in your ridiculous schemes," Maria snapped, her protective instincts flaring. She'd seen too many of Wayne's plans go up in smoke, and the thought of her daughter being pulled into another one made her heart ache.

But Selena wasn't having it. "It's not ridiculous," she insisted, her eyes shining with the kind of enthusiasm only a teenager could muster for such an outlandish idea. "It's kinda cool!"

Wayne couldn't help but smile at his daughter's support, a glimmer of his old charm showing through. But the smile faded quickly under Maria's withering glare.

"It is not cool," Maria said, her voice low and intense. "It is a childish fantasy to think you can just come to El Paso and find gold." The words hung in the air, heavy with the weight of past disappointments and broken promises.

Wayne leaned forward, his voice taking on a desperate edge. "If I found this treasure, it would help with the money problems here." The unspoken struggles of their daily life seemed to fill the spaces between his words.

Maria's response was quick and sharp. "We are doing just fine."

"No we're not." Selena's quiet words cut through the room like a knife, silencing both her parents.

Maria turned to her daughter, shock evident on her face. "What?"

Selena took a deep breath, years of pent-up frustration and worry spilling out. "Come on, mom. I know it's been hard on us. I want to go to college, but we can't afford it." The pain in her voice was unmistakable, a young woman watching her dreams slip away in the face of harsh reality.

Maria's expression softened for a moment before hardening again as she turned back to Wayne. "We can manage without him and his fantasy treasure hunts."

"That's not true," Selena countered, her voice gaining strength. "If Wayne...Dad finds this gold, our problems would be gone!"

The hope in her daughter's voice seemed to fuel Maria's anger. She turned to Wayne, her words dripping with sarcasm. "What are you gonna do, Wayne? Google 'Find me some missing Gold?'"

Wayne looked up at her, confusion etched across his weathered face. "Google?"

Maria threw her hands up in exasperation. "Oh my God, Wayne. Get with the times. You know, online searching? Googling? It's as simple as A B C!"

Something seemed to click in Wayne's mind. He stood up abruptly, a new energy in his movements. "You're right!"

"Wait, what are you —" Maria started, but Selena was already on her feet.

"Where are we going?" Selena asked, excitement building in her voice.

Wayne turned back to his daughter, a spark of adventure in his eyes that had been missing for far too long. "To the Google place."

"Google place?" Maria echoed, disbelief coloring her words.

"I'm coming with you!" Selena declared, already moving towards the door.

Maria stood up, her voice rising in alarm. "Now wait one minute."

For once, Wayne seemed to hesitate. He turned to Selena, concern creeping into his expression. "I don't think that's a good idea."

"For once I agree with this man," Maria said, relief evident in her voice.

But Selena wasn't backing down. Her eyes blazed with determination as she faced her parents. "Too bad, Dad! We need the money, and nothing is gonna stop us. Not Mom, not the drug cartel, not anything!"

Maria exclaimed, "What drug cartel?!" She found herself alone in the dining room, her world turned upside down. She called after them, her voice a mix of shock and concern,

The sound of a car engine starting up outside was her only answer, leaving her to grapple with the sudden, chaotic turn of events. Maria stood at the kitchen window, her mind miles away. Now, Maria feared history was repeating itself with their daughter, Selena. She glanced at the collection of artifacts adorning their living room shelves. And now, she saw that same glimmer of excitement in Selena's eyes whenever Wayne regaled her with tales of hidden treasures and lost cities.

Maria dried her hands, her heart heavy. Even at her age, she knew that Selena was at a crossroads. She had her father's fierce intelligence and insatiable curiosity,

141

but also his recklessness, his disregard for consequences.

"Dios mío," Maria whispered, crossing herself. "Please don't let her follow this foolish path."

She once loved Wayne, but she couldn't bear to watch her daughter throw away her future chasing myths and legends. The world was dangerous enough without seeking out its darkest corners and most jealously guarded secrets. Maybe it was time to show Selena that real treasure – love, family, a life well-lived – wasn't buried in some long-forgotten tomb.

The morning sun beat down on the bustling streets of El Paso as Wayne's beat-up sedan pulled into the parking lot of the city's main library. The imposing brick building stood before them, its windows glinting in the harsh light.

Wayne turned to Selena, his face alight with excitement and a touch of naivety. "The Google place!" he announced triumphantly, as if he'd just discovered the holy grail of information.

Selena couldn't help but shake her head in wonder. Her newfound father's lack of technological knowledge was both endearing and slightly concerning. She bit back a smile, not wanting to dampen his enthusiasm.

"Um, Dad," she started, the word still feeling foreign on her tongue, "I don't think that's exactly how Google works."

But Wayne was already unbuckling his seatbelt, his energy palpable. "Come on, kiddo! Let's go find our treasure!"

As they climbed out of the car, Selena couldn't shake the feeling that this misguided library trip was just the beginning of a much larger adventure. The mention of the drug cartel still echoed in her mind, a dangerous undercurrent to their treasure hunting fantasy. She followed Wayne up the library steps, equal parts excited and apprehensive. Whatever lay ahead, she knew their lives would never be the same. The library was cool and quiet, a stark contrast to the scorching El Paso day outside. Wayne marched purposefully towards the card catalog, his fingers dancing over the worn edges of the drawers.

Selena trailed behind him, curiosity piqued. "What are we looking for?" she asked, her voice hushed in the library's silence.

"We are looking for Franklin mountain maps," Wayne replied, flipping through the cards with practiced ease. He paused, a hint of nostalgia in his voice. "This is the Dewey Decimal System. Do they teach this to you kids anymore?"

Selena couldn't help but smirk. "I know what the Dewey Decimal System is. I just don't need to use it!" Her tone was a mix of exasperation and amusement at her father's outdated methods.

Wayne chuckled, closing the drawer. "Follow me," he said, leading the way to a far corner of the library.

They stopped before a shelf of oversized books. Wayne pulled out a hefty tome, its pages filled with detailed maps of the Franklin Mountains. As he flipped through, Selena leaned in, her eyes scanning the intricate contours and markings.

Suddenly, Wayne stopped on a page, his finger pointing to a large letter on the side of a mountain. "As easy as A B C," he said, a triumphant grin spreading across his face.

Selena's eyes widened in recognition. "That's my old school... Coronado High!" she exclaimed, her finger jabbing at the 'C' on the mountainside.

Wayne turned to Selena, surprise evident in his features. "What are you talking about?"

"My school! Coronado High. Everyone knows this... except you obviously," Selena explained, a hint of teenage superiority in her voice.

Wayne's eyes lit up with interest. "Actually, I have heard of Coronado High. Tell me what you know."

144

Selena launched into an explanation, her words tumbling out in excitement. "Each of our high schools have a letter on the side of the mountain. At least the ones that are cool enough to have done it."

"So this letter is associated with your school?" Wayne pressed, his mind clearly working overtime.

"Yeah, it was big in my church," Selena added, not quite understanding the significance of her words.

Wayne's expression shifted, a mix of excitement and determination settling over his features. Without another word, he snapped the book shut and began leading Selena out of the library. Selena felt a thrill of anticipation. They had come looking for Google and instead found a potential clue to the treasure. She couldn't help but wonder what other surprises lay in store for them on this unconventional father-daughter adventure.

The library doors swung shut behind them as they stepped back into the blazing El Paso sun, the first piece of their treasure map puzzle secured in Wayne's grip. Selena's heart raced as she pored over the worn map spread across her desk, her father's stories echoing in her mind. The thrill of potential discovery tingled through her veins, a heady mixture of excitement and fear that left her breathless.

Selena imagining herself trekking through uncharted wilderness, deciphering ancient clues, always one step

145

ahead of danger. The idea both terrified and exhilarated her. "What if I'm not cut out for this?" she thought to herself, doubt creeping in. She thought of her father's scars, the haunted look in his eyes when he spoke of close calls. Treasure hunting wasn't just about glory and gold – it was about facing the darkness, both in the world and within oneself.

But then she remembered the way Wayne's eyes lit up when he described unearthing a long-lost artifact, the rush of solving a centuries-old puzzle. It was more than just adventure; it was about preserving history, uncovering truths buried by time. Selena's gaze drifted again. Could she handle the weight of this newfound legacy? The constant vigilance, the split-second decisions that meant the difference between life and death?

Selena closed her eyes, imagining herself standing at the entrance of a hidden cave, torch in hand, heart pounding. The unknown stretched before her, full of promise and peril. Part of her wanted to run, to choose a safe, predictable life. But a stronger part yearned to step into that darkness, to test herself against the mysteries of the world.

"I could be great," she murmured, a mix of hope and uncertainty in her voice. "Or I could lose everything."

~Chapter 15~

Who is Pastor Oro?

Wayne burst into the hotel room like a man possessed, his eyes gleaming with the fervor of discovery. He unfurled a map across the bed, snatching up a red marker as Selena followed him inside, bewildered.

"What are you doing?" she asked, watching as her father's hands flew across the paper.

"The church was big in your school?" Wayne questioned, his focus intense.

Selena nodded, recalling fragments of conversation she'd overheard. "People would talk about how, back in the day, the church sponsored things out there, showing school spirit and all."

Wayne's excitement grew palpable. "And those schools had letters on the mountains, right?"

"Yeah, I guess," Selena replied, still not grasping the significance. "Why?"

Wayne spun around, yanking a school roster from the cork board. "Name off the schools that had letters," he demanded.

Selena started listing the schools as Wayne scribbled furiously, his pen dancing across the map. "There's Burgess, Irvin, Eastwood...let me think." As she continued, Wayne started writing the first letters of selective names.

Wayne looked at the letters on hand, five in total- A, C, E, B, and I.

Suddenly, he stepped back, his gaze shifting to the mysterious kapok cloth they'd found earlier. Selena watched, fascinated, as the pieces seemed to click into place in her father's mind.

"The church had this kapok cloth hidden in the statue," Wayne said, his voice tinged with awe.

With a flourish, he rearranged the letters on a sheet, spelling out "CEIBA" on the corkboard. "The church sponsored these five schools. Those letters spell Ceiba, which is another word for 'Kapok'!"

Selena's eyes widened. "Cool!" she exclaimed, caught up in the thrill of the discovery.

But Wayne's expression darkened. "No, not cool. The Spanish missions were already looking for the treasure. They must have been using the letters to mark out exactly where they had already searched."

A chill ran down Selena's spine as the implications sank in. "Why did they stop?"

Wayne's next words fell like lead in the room: "I think they already found the gold."

Selena's heart sank. "So you mean there's nothing for us to find?"

Wayne paused, his expression unreadable. "I gotta go see a man about a drink," he said abruptly, heading for the door. As he swung it open, they were both startled to find Elizabeth standing outside, her presence an unexpected twist in their unfolding adventure.

The room fell silent, the air thick with tension and unanswered questions. What did Elizabeth's appearance mean for their treasure hunt? And if the

Spanish missions had already found the gold, what were Wayne and Selena really chasing?

As father and daughter exchanged a look of surprise and apprehension, it was clear that their journey was far from over — and that it might be leading them into deeper, more dangerous waters than either had anticipated.

The tension in the room spiked as Elizabeth stood in the doorway, a small piece of luggage in her hand. "Hi Wayne," she said, her voice a mix of surprise and something harder to define.

Wayne's face fell. "Oh God," he muttered, the words barely audible.

Selena looked between the two adults, confusion etched on her face. "Who is that?" she asked, her tone wary.

Elizabeth's gaze snapped to Selena, her eyes narrowing. "Who is THAT?" Elizabeth echoed, her voice sharp as she turned back to Wayne.

Her mind raced, piecing together a narrative she didn't want to believe. Wayne's late nights, his secretive phone calls, the way he'd been distant lately. It all seemed to crystallize into a sickening realization.

"No," Elizabeth whispered, her voice barely audible. "He wouldn't..."

But the evidence was right in front of her. The girl stirred, her eyes fluttering open. She looked startled, then confused, clearly not expecting to see Elizabeth there.

Elizabeth's heart pounded in her chest, a mix of anger and devastation threatening to overwhelm her. How could Wayne do this? And with someone so young? It was more than betrayal – it was predatory.

She took a step back, her hand shaking as she fumbled for her phone. Should she confront Wayne? Call the police? Her mind spun with horrible possibilities.

"I'm such a fool," Elizabeth thought, fighting back tears. She'd trusted Wayne, believed in him. Now, faced with this unimaginable scene, she questioned everything about their relationship.

Elizabeth's mind raced with questions. Who was that girl? And most pressingly – what was she going to do now?

Wayne hesitated, trapped between the two women. He took a deep breath, as if steeling himself. "Liz, honey... she's my daughter."

The word 'daughter' seemed to echo in the suddenly silent room. Elizabeth's eyes widened in shock. "Daughter?!" she exclaimed, her voice rising an octave.

Selena, sensing the growing tension, tried to diffuse it with a touch of humor. "I know, I just found out myself!" she said with a nervous laugh.

But Wayne was already moving, pushing past Elizabeth in a rush. "I'm on to something here. I have to go!" he called over his shoulder, leaving the two women staring after him in disbelief.

Wayne's footsteps faded down the hallway. Elizabeth turned back to Selena, her eyes searching the young woman's face. "Are you REALLY his daughter?" she asked, skepticism clear in her voice.

Selena, feeling uncomfortable under Elizabeth's scrutiny, resorted to nonverbal communication. She scrunched up her face in an exaggerated expression of disgust, shaking her head vigorously to dispel any notion that she and Wayne could be anything other than father and daughter.

The silent exchange hung in the air between them, laden with unspoken questions and barely concealed tensions. Selena found herself wondering just who this Elizabeth was, and what her presence meant for the treasure hunt - and for her newfound relationship with her father.

The two women stood there, sizing each other up. Selena couldn't shake the feeling that their adventure had just taken yet another unexpected turn. With Wayne gone and this stranger at the door, she realized she was now navigating uncharted waters - both in terms of the treasure hunt and her own complicated family dynamics.

The sun beat down mercilessly on the ancient stones of the Spanish mission as Wayne approached, his breath coming in short gasps from his hurried journey. His eyes locked onto a religious figure sweeping the front entrance, someone that he had not met on this adventure.

Padre Oro looked up from his task, his weathered face hardening into a mask of stern disapproval. Before Wayne could even open his mouth, the priest's words cut through the air like a whip.

"Mister, I know what you are trying to do, and this is not in keeping with God's work. Leave immediately!" Padre Oro's voice was filled with barely contained anger, his knuckles whitening as he gripped the broom handle.

Wayne faltered, taken aback by the hostile reception. Confusion clouded his features as he stammered, "I'm looking for Padre Gonzalez."

The priest's expression didn't soften. If anything, it grew even more severe. "Mister Gonzalez is no longer a servant of God here," he stated flatly, his tone brooking no argument.

Without warning, Padre Oro raised his broom, brandishing it like a weapon. "Now leave and don't come back!" he commanded, his voice rising.

Wayne instinctively raised his hands in a placating gesture, backing away from the irate priest. His mind raced, trying to piece together this unexpected turn of events. What had happened to Padre Gonzalez? And why was Padre Oro so adamant about driving him away?

As he retreated from the mission, Wayne couldn't shake the feeling that he'd stumbled upon something far more complex - and potentially dangerous - than a simple treasure hunt. The priest's reaction suggested that the secrets buried in El Paso's past were not going to give themselves up easily.

With one last glance at the imposing facade of the mission, Wayne turned and walked away, his steps quick but his mind slow with the weight of new questions. He had come seeking answers, but had only found more mysteries. As the mission receded behind him, he knew that his quest was far from over - and that the stakes might be higher than he had ever imagined.

The cool air of the hotel lobby washed over Wayne as he entered, a welcome respite from the scorching El Paso heat. His mind was still churning with questions from his encounter at the mission when a voice cut through his thoughts.

"Mr. Braddock!" The hotel clerk waved, catching Wayne's attention.

Wayne paused, turning towards the counter. "Yes?" he asked, his voice tinged with weariness and curiosity.

The clerk extended a package towards him. "This came in for you," he said, a hint of intrigue in his voice.

Wayne nodded his thanks, taking the package. His fingers worked quickly to open it, revealing a book on metalworking. A note protruded from between the pages, drawing his attention. He flipped to the marked page, his eyes widening as they fell upon a detailed design of a mining cart.

With growing anticipation, Wayne unfolded the letter that had accompanied the book. As he read, the blood seemed to drain from his face:

> "Braddock, Not all of us died in that plane crash. With my failing health, I cannot hold this secret anymore. The treasure was out there. Signed, Howe"

Wayne's hands trembled slightly as he lowered the letter. His gaze returned to the mining cart design, seeing it now with new eyes. Slowly, he rotated the book, studying every detail with intense focus.

A smile began to spread across his face, a mix of excitement and determination replacing the confusion of moments before. Without a word to the curious clerk, Wayne turned on his heel and strode out of the hotel, his steps purposeful and quick.

Wayne felt a surge of renewed energy. The treasure hunt that had seemed to hit a dead end at the mission now pulsed with new life. Howe's words echoed in his mind: "The treasure was out there."

~ Chapter 16 ~
Back to the Mountains

The El Paso sun beat down on him once more as he emerged onto the street, but Wayne barely noticed. His mind was already racing ahead, piecing together this new information with what he already knew. The mining cart, the crash, the hidden treasure - it all seemed to be coming together.

With each step, Wayne's determination grew. He had come to El Paso chasing a dream, a possibility. Now, with Howe's confirmation, that dream felt tantalizingly close to reality. Whatever obstacles lay ahead - be they angry priests, skeptical family members, or dangerous rivals - Wayne was more resolved than ever to see this through to the end.

The sun hung high in the cloudless sky as Wayne made his way along the rugged mountainside. His boots crunched against loose gravel and scrub, the sound echoing in the quiet air. The path he followed was barely visible, more of a game trail than anything made by human hands.

Rounding a bend, the landscape suddenly opened up before him. Wayne found himself in a clearing, his breath catching in his throat at the sight. Scattered across the ground were countless white rocks, their pale surfaces gleaming in the harsh sunlight.

For a moment, Wayne stood motionless, his eyes sweeping across the scene. Then, slowly, a smile spread across his face as realization dawned. He wasn't just standing in a random collection of stones. No, this was something far more significant.

He was standing in the middle of the "A" - the very same letter he had seen on the map back in the library. The white rocks had been carefully arranged to form the massive letter, visible from miles away but nearly indistinguishable up close without the proper perspective.

Wayne's heart raced with excitement. This wasn't just a school spirit symbol or a landmark. It was a clue - a piece of the puzzle he'd been trying to solve. The Spanish missions, the treasure, Howe's letter - it all seemed to be coming together here on this sun-baked mountainside.

He took a deep breath, savoring the moment. The dry desert air filled his lungs, carrying with it the scent of dust and adventure. Wayne knew he was on the right track now. The treasure was out there, just as Howe had said, and he was one step closer to finding it.

With renewed determination, Wayne set off again. He moved with purpose now, his eyes alert for any other signs or markers that might lead him further along this dangerous and exciting path. As he left the "A" behind, disappearing once more into the rugged terrain, Wayne couldn't help but feel that he was on the verge of something big.

The mountain kept its secrets close, but Wayne Braddock was more determined than ever to uncover them. With each step, he moved closer to the truth - and to the treasure that had brought him to El Paso in the first place.

The harsh midday sun beat down on Wayne as he ascended the mountainside, his breathing labored but determined. The rocky terrain challenged every step, but he pressed on, driven by an unwavering sense of purpose.

Passing the crash site, memories of his previous visit flooded back. The scorched earth and scattered debris served as a grim reminder of the tragedy that had occurred here. But today, Wayne wasn't here to mourn. He was here to uncover the truth.

Wayne pulled out the medallion he'd been carrying. Its weight felt significant in his hand, not just physically but with the promise of what it might reveal. Wayne turned it upside down, his eyes narrowing as he held it up against the horizon.

For a moment, nothing seemed to happen. Then, as he slowly panned across the jagged skyline, something clicked into place. The intricate design on the medallion suddenly aligned perfectly with the mountain peaks before him, revealing a notch that had been hidden in plain sight. Wayne's heart raced. This was it. The medallion wasn't just a trinket or a red herring. It was a key, a map leading him to the next step of his journey.

A smile spread across his weathered face, a mix of triumph and anticipation. Without hesitation, he pocketed the medallion and set his sights on the newly discovered notch. Each step towards the mountain top felt charged with possibility.

Wayne navigated the treacherous slope, his mind whirling with questions. What would he find at the notch? How deep did this mystery go? And who else might be on the trail of this long-lost treasure?

The path grew steeper, more challenging, but Wayne barely noticed. His focus was entirely on what lay ahead. He was no longer just chasing a dream or a rumor. He was following a tangible lead, one that promised to unravel the secrets that had brought him to El Paso.

With the sun at his back and the notch growing ever closer, Wayne pressed on. He was more certain than ever that he was on the right track. Whatever awaited him at the top of this mountain, he was ready to face it head-on.

The adventure that had begun with a cryptic clue and a desperate hope was now leading him to what could be the discovery of a lifetime. And Wayne Braddock, treasure hunter and newfound father, was determined to see it through to the end.

The sun had begun its slow descent towards the horizon as Wayne crested the mountain notch. His muscles ached from the climb, but the thrill of discovery pushed him forward. As he reached the top, he paused for a moment, catching his breath and surveying the landscape that stretched out before him.

The view from the notch was breathtaking. To the west, the familiar terrain of El Paso sprawled out, a patchwork of urban development and desert scrubland. But it was the eastern face of the mountain that now captured Wayne's attention.

With careful, deliberate steps, he began to make his way down the other side. The terrain here was different - more rugged, less travelled. Each footfall had to be calculated, the loose scree threatening to send him tumbling with any misstep.

Descending, Wayne's keen eyes scanned the landscape, searching for any sign of the treasure he sought. The eastern face of the mountain was bathed in long shadows, creating a stark contrast of light and dark that made every feature stand out in sharp relief.

The air felt different on this side, cooler and somehow charged with potential. Wayne couldn't shake the feeling that he was crossing a threshold, not just physically but metaphorically. He was entering uncharted territory, both in terms of the land and his quest.

With each step down the eastern slope, Wayne felt a growing sense of anticipation. What secrets did this side of the mountain hold? Was he the first treasure hunter to make it this far, or were there others who had stood where he now stood?

Making his way down the mountainside, Wayne's mind raced with possibilities. The medallion had led him here for a reason. Now, on this less-explored face of the mountain, he felt closer than ever to unraveling the mystery that had brought him to El Paso.

The sun continued its descent, casting long shadows across the rugged terrain. Wayne pressed on, his determination unwavering. Whatever lay ahead - be it the treasure he sought or more clues to follow - he was ready to face it.

With the notch now behind him and a new landscape stretching out before him, Wayne Braddock took a deep breath of the cooling air. He was one step closer to his goal, and nothing was going to stop him now.

Wayne made his way down the eastern slope, his eyes caught sight of something that made his heart skip a beat. There, partially hidden by overgrown vegetation and weathered rocks, was the entrance to a mine shaft. It was so well concealed that he might have missed it entirely if not for the slanting rays of the setting sun catching on a bit of worn metal.

Wayne approached cautiously, his senses on high alert. As he drew closer, he noticed a faded glyph painted on the side of the entrance. It was a tree, its branches spreading out in an intricate pattern. The sight of it sent a jolt of excitement through him. This had to be more than just an abandoned mine - it was a sign, a marker left behind by those who had come before. Wayne recognized it immediately, as once again he had come across a kapok symbol.

Wayne cleared away some of the debris obstructing the entrance. He found a gap just wide enough for him to squeeze through. Taking a deep breath, he slipped inside, the cool darkness of the mine shaft enveloping him.

Wayne pulled out his flashlight, its beam cutting through the gloom. The air was thick with the scent of earth and old timber. He moved forward slowly, his footsteps echoing in the confined space.

Just a few feet in, Wayne's light fell upon another glyph painted on the wall. His breath caught in his throat as he recognized the symbol - it was another kapok, the very same image that had been central to his quest from the beginning.

Wayne's mind raced. The kapok glyph, the hidden entrance, the eastern face of the mountain - it all pointed to one thrilling conclusion. He wasn't just exploring an old mine; he was standing at the threshold of something far more significant.

Wayne stared at the kapok glyph, feeling a surge of anticipation. Whatever lay deeper in this mine shaft, he was certain it held the key to the treasure he'd been seeking. The Spanish missions, the cryptic clues, the dangerous journey - it had all led him here, to this hidden entrance on the eastern face of the mountain.

Wayne adjusted his grip on the flashlight and took a step deeper into the mine. The darkness ahead seemed to hold a thousand secrets, and he was ready to uncover them all.

The darkness of the mine shaft enveloped Wayne as he ventured deeper, his flashlight beam cutting through the gloom like a knife. The air was thick with dust and the musty scent of ages past. Each step echoed ominously in the confined space, adding to the tension that gripped him.

Suddenly, his light fell upon something that made his heart leap - a treasure chest. It sat there in the darkness, as if waiting just for him. Wayne's excitement mounted as he approached, his hands trembling slightly as he reached for the lid.

With a creak that seemed to reverberate through the entire mine, the chest opened. Wayne's eyes widened as he saw the glint of gold coins within. For a moment, euphoria washed over him. He had done it. He had found the treasure.

But as he reached out to touch the coins, his elation turned to bitter disappointment. The gold was fake - nothing more than painted props left to fool treasure hunters like himself. Wayne's shoulders sagged as the reality of the situation sank in.

Before he could fully process this setback, a blinding light suddenly flooded his vision. Wayne recoiled, throwing his hands up to shield his eyes from the harsh glare.

A voice cut through the darkness, smooth and sardonic. "Congratulations Mr. Braddock. I think you found what you were looking for."

Wayne squinted against the light, trying to make out the speaker. But before he could respond or react, he felt a presence behind him. There was a sharp pain at the base of his skull, and then... darkness.

As Wayne's unconscious form crumpled to the ground, the man with the light - Decker - spoke again. "Okay, let's get him out of here."

The soldier who had struck Wayne nodded silently, moving to lift the treasure hunter's limp body. As they dragged Wayne out of the mine shaft, the fake treasure chest sat forgotten, a cruel reminder of how close he had come to unraveling the mystery - and how dangerous this game had truly become.

The darkness of the mine seemed to close in behind them, swallowing up the scene and leaving only questions in its wake. Who were these men? What did they want with Wayne? And most importantly - if the treasure in the chest was fake, where was the real gold hidden?

Wayne was carried away into an uncertain fate, unconscious to realize the true depth of the conspiracy he had stumbled into began to reveal itself. The adventure had taken a dark turn, and the stakes were now higher than ever.

~ Chapter 17 ~
Secret Government Twists

Wayne's head throbbed as consciousness slowly returned. The first thing he noticed was the biting cold of metal against his wrists – handcuffs, tight enough to chafe. As his vision cleared, the enormity of his predicament came into focus.

He was seated in a steel chair, its legs bolted to the concrete floor of what appeared to be a vast, dilapidated military warehouse. The air hung heavy with the scent of rust and damp. Dim light filtered through grimy windows high above, casting long shadows across the cavernous space.

Wayne's eyes darted upward, his stomach tightening as he spotted the armed guards. They patrolled the metal catwalks and rafters, their rifles glinting ominously in the half-light. Their faces were obscured by balaclavas, adding to the surreal, nightmarish quality of the scene.

Along the walls, banks of computer equipment hummed and blinked, their purpose a mystery that only heightened Wayne's growing sense of dread. This was no ordinary hideout or interrogation site. Whatever was happening here, it was sophisticated, well-funded, and utterly outside his realm of experience.

"Is this it?" Wayne thought, a chill running down his spine that had nothing to do with the cold. "Is this where it all ends?"

He'd been in tight spots before, but this felt different. The clinical efficiency of the setup, the sheer manpower involved – it all pointed to an operation far beyond simple revenge or territorialism.

Wayne tested his restraints, wincing at the metal's unyielding grip. His mind raced, trying to piece together how he'd ended up here, who could be behind this. But the gaps in his memory only added to his mounting fear.

Footsteps echoed from somewhere in the shadows. Wayne steeled himself. Whether this was to be an execution or something even worse, he was determined to face it with whatever dignity he could muster.

Before him stood a man in a white doctor's jacket, flanked by two armed guards. The walls were adorned with "Area 51" signs, and the military personnel wore tags bearing the same ominous designation.

"Where am I?" Wayne croaked, his throat dry and his voice hoarse.

In response, the man before him - Decker - held up a badge. The Area 51 logo glared back at Wayne, sending a chill down his spine.

"What am I doing in Nevada?" Wayne asked, confusion and fear warring in his mind.

Decker's voice was cool, almost clinical. "You are here because you have stumbled into a dire situation that you should not be a part of."

Wayne's mind raced, trying to piece together the events that had led him here. "What are you talking about?"

"This fine country has secrets," Decker replied, his tone measured. "Secrets we like to keep. You know about secrets, don't you?"

"Secrets?" Wayne echoed, a sinking feeling in his gut.

169

Decker's eyes narrowed. "Yes, like what happened to the Spanish gold from the 1700s. Those types of secrets."

The pieces began to fall into place in Wayne's mind. "The military took the Spanish gold?" he asked, disbelief coloring his voice.

"Yes, about sixty years ago," Decker confirmed with an eerie laugh.

Wayne's world seemed to tilt on its axis. The treasure he had been seeking, the mystery he had devoted so much of his life to solving - it had been in the hands of the government all along. The implications were staggering.

Bound and at the mercy of these shadowy figures, Wayne realized that his treasure hunt had led him into something far bigger and more dangerous than he could have ever imagined. The hangar suddenly felt oppressive, the weight of hidden truths and government secrets pressing down on him.

"What do you want with me?" Wayne asked. He wondered how he was going to get out of this? As Decker loomed over him, Wayne knew that the answers to these questions could very well determine whether he lived or died.

Decker's laughter died away, leaving an eerie silence in its wake. Wayne's heart pounded in his chest as he watched Decker reach into his jacket pocket. The glint of metal made Wayne's breath catch in his throat.

"Funny you should mention that," Decker said, his voice low and dangerous.

In one fluid motion, Decker produced a handgun in his right hand. The overhead lights glinted off its polished surface. Wayne's eyes were drawn to Decker's left hand, which was curled into a tight fist, concealing something.

Before Wayne could react, he felt the cold, hard press of the gun barrel against his temple. A bead of sweat trickled down his forehead as Decker leaned in close, his breath hot on Wayne's ear.

"I'm going to give you a choice," Decker whispered.

Panic surged through Wayne's body. His mind raced, weighing his options in a fraction of a second. The gun in Decker's right hand was an obvious threat, but what was in Decker's other hand? A grenade? A syringe? His survival instinct kicked in.

"Left hand! Left hand! Left hand!" Wayne screamed, his voice echoing off the warehouse walls.

Decker glanced down at his closed fist, a hint of amusement playing across his features. "Are you sure?" he asked, raising an eyebrow.

Wayne nodded frantically, words tumbling out of his mouth. "Of course! I'd rather be punched than shot, but not my teeth!"

To Wayne's surprise, Decker burst into laughter again. The gun wavered slightly, but remained pressed against Wayne's head.

"You have it all wrong, Mr. Braddock," Decker said, shaking his head. "I'm not going to hit you, but you did make the right choice."

Slowly, agonizingly, Decker pulled the gun away from Wayne's head. Wayne exhaled sharply, not realizing he'd been holding his breath.

"You understand that if you reveal any military secrets, you will be treated as a threat to the nation, and as such, a felon," Decker continued, his tone serious once more. "How does prison sound?"

Wayne swallowed hard, his mouth dry. "Not good," he croaked. "I won't tell anyone!"

A smile spread across Decker's face, but it didn't reach his eyes. He uncurled his left hand, revealing a small, gleaming object. Wayne's eyes widened as he recognized the unmistakable sheen of gold.

"Then your prize is life, and this small token of appreciation for what you have accomplished," Decker said, holding out a gold bullion. "But if you should talk..." He raised the gun again, letting the threat hang in the air.

Decker placed the gold piece in Wayne's shirt pocket. It was heavier than he expected, its weight a tangible proof of the incredible story he had pieced together. As the reality of the situation sank in, a mix of awe and terror washed over him.

Decker leaned in close once more, his voice barely above a whisper. "Don't make me regret leaving you alive, my son."

Wayne nodded frantically, his chin quivering slightly. The weight of everything seemed to anchor him to this surreal moment.

Decker studied Wayne's face for a long moment, as if committing every detail to memory. Then, apparently satisfied with what he saw, he turned his head slightly to the side. Wayne followed his gaze and noticed for the first time a soldier standing silently in the shadows.

With a barely perceptible nod from Decker, the soldier sprang into action. Before Wayne could react, rough hands grabbed him from behind. He felt the coarse fabric of a blindfold being pulled over his eyes, plunging him into darkness.

"Wait, what's happening?" Wayne cried out, his voice tinged with panic.

But no answer came. He felt himself being lifted off his feet, the soldier's grip firm and unyielding. The gold bullion was still clutched in his hand, a small comfort in the chaos.

Wayne's other senses heightened in the darkness. He could smell the musty air of the warehouse, hear the echoing footsteps as he was carried away. The soldier's breathing was steady and controlled, a stark contrast to Wayne's own ragged gasps.

As they moved, Wayne tried to keep track of their path, but soon became disoriented. Left turn, right turn, straight ahead - it all blurred together in his mind.

Finally, he felt a rush of cool air on his face. They must be outside now, he realized. The sounds changed - the echo of the warehouse replaced by the ambient noise of the night. A military jeep door opened, and Wayne was unceremoniously deposited onto what felt like a back seat.

~ Chapter 18 ~

The Real Culprits

The sun beat down mercilessly on the weathered corrugated metal of the warehouse. An old jeep, its olive-drab paint faded and chipped, sat in the gravelly lot outside. The air shimmered with heat, distorting the view of the distant mountains. At the front entrance, a military sentry stood at attention, his face impassive beneath the brim of his cap. His eyes constantly scanned the surroundings, alert for any sign of movement in this desolate landscape.

Inside the jeep, Wayne sat rigid in the back seat. The rough fabric of the blindfold scratched against his skin, and beads of sweat trickled down his temples. His hands trembled slightly. The leather seat beneath him was hot to the touch, and the air inside the vehicle was stifling.

With a crunch of gravel, the driver's door opened and closed. Wayne felt the jeep shift as the soldier settled into the driver's seat. The key turned in the ignition, and the engine sputtered to life with a roar that seemed deafening in the quiet desert air. The jeep began to move, lurching slightly over the uneven ground. Wayne tried to orient himself. Left? Right? He had no way of knowing.

In the warehouse doorway, Decker stood watching the jeep's departure. His face was set in a grim expression, eyes narrowed against the glare of the sun. As the vehicle kicked up a cloud of dust, obscuring its path, a small smile played at the corners of Decker's mouth. The jeep's engine noise faded into the distance, leaving only the sound of the wind whistling around the corners of the warehouse. Decker remained in the doorway for a long moment, as if contemplating the events that had just unfolded. Finally, with a slight nod to himself, he turned and disappeared back into the shadows of the building.

A sentry from afar lowered his weapon, breathing a sigh of relief that he could soon seize the charade that had confused their recent captor. As the warehouse door clanged shut behind him, Decker's shoulders sagged with relief. He turned to face the group of men standing in the cavernous space, their faces a mixture of anticipation and wariness. With a fluid motion, Decker shrugged off his lab coat. Beneath it, the crisp lines of a missionary's uniform were revealed, a stark contrast to his previous stern scientist demeanor.

"Well," he said, his voice echoing slightly in the vast room, "I pray to God that this stops Mr. Braddock and his hunt for the gold." He paused, a hint of uncertainty creeping into his tone. "Do you think he fell for the military conspiracy?"

From the shadows, two figures emerged. One was Trujillo, also clad in a missionary's garb, his face impassive. Beside him walked Padre Oro, his eyes sharp and calculating as they swept over the group of disrobed soldier-padres.

"I think so," Trujillo said, his gaze settling on Decker while standing next to Padre Oro.

A smile tugged at Oro's lips. "Maybe more convincing than the drug cartel angle?"

Trujillo stepped forward, his face a mask of seriousness. "Oro, you never know what manner of influence works on any specific individual. I tried the most violent way, though I personally did not enjoy it."

"Not even a little?" Decker's eyebrow arched in amusement.

A smile flickered across Trujillo's face, breaking his stoic façade for a moment. "Braddock actually found our imposter mine. Quite impressive."

Oro's voice cut through the air, bringing them back to the matter at hand. His tone grew grave as he continued, "Braddock only kept it up to help his struggling family. Just to be safe that he doesn't come hunting again, let's provide Braddock's daughter with a nice scholarship, to help alleviate their family's financial burdens."

"Agreed," Decker nodded, his expression thoughtful.

His voice then lowered, taking on a more ominous tone. "So that leaves this one final loose end."

As one, the men turned to face the far corner of the warehouse. There, hunched in a metal folding chair, sat Padre Gonzalez. His face was pale, eyes darting nervously between the men who now regarded him with cool calculation.

"What to do with our little instigator?" Decker mused, his earlier warmth completely gone.

A thin smile spread across Oro's face as he continued, "Oh, I believe there is plenty of good work to be done in Antarctica, for the sake of our lord and savior, of course."

The words hung in the air, heavy with implied threat. In his corner, Padre Gonzalez seemed to shrink even smaller, the weight of his actions - and their consequences - visibly crushing him.

Padre Oro paused for a moment, his demeanor becoming more authoritative. "Wayne Braddock may have found the clues our church placed years ago, to lure treasure hunters on false trails. More may be out there, and it does not change the fact that the real gold remains undiscovered. And by decree we will continue to look for it ourselves."

As silence fell over the warehouse, the true nature of their elaborate deception became clear. The military, the gold, the threats - all a carefully orchestrated performance to protect a secret that ran far deeper than Braddock could have ever imagined.

Wayne Braddock sank into the worn armchair of the cheap hotel room, his body aching, mind reeling from the events of the past few days. Elizabeth perched on the edge of the bed, her face a mixture of relief and lingering worry as she watched him.

"I still can't believe you're okay," she said softly, reaching out to touch his hand. "When you didn't come back, I thought..."

Wayne managed a weak smile. "I'm alive, that's what matters." He glanced around the room, as if still expecting to see armed guards in the shadows. "But, I was so close, Liz. The gold was practically in my grasp."

Elizabeth's brow furrowed. "The gold? Wayne, you were held in a secret military base. Shouldn't we be more concerned about that?"

He nodded absently, his mind still on the lost treasure. "You're right, of course. It's just... all that work, all those risks, and we came up empty-handed."

"We?" Elizabeth raised an eyebrow. "I think you mean you, Wayne. I told you this was dangerous."

Wayne leaned forward, wincing slightly. "I know, I know. But you don't understand. The things I saw there, the questions they asked – this is bigger than just some lost Spanish gold. There's something else going on, something huge."

Elizabeth stood up, pacing the small room. "No, Wayne. No more. You promised this would be the last time. You promised we'd settle down after this."

Wayne watched her, feeling the familiar pull between the life he'd promised her and the mysteries that still called to him. He was thankful to be alive, to be here with her. But the thrill of the unknown, the lure of discovery – it still whispered to him, as enticing as ever.

"You're right," he said finally, standing to embrace her.

Elizabeth moved about, starting to fold and pack clothes into an open suitcase on the bed.

"I am so glad that you have finally decided to end this silly treasure hunt," Elizabeth chattered, her voice a mix of relief and excitement. "Now you can take me on a nice long vacation. I understand that money may be a little tight, but I think that together we can afford something nice, maybe off of the coast of Jamaica."

Wayne stood before his research board, methodically removing pins and papers. His movements were automatic, his mind elsewhere. Elizabeth's words washed over him, barely registering. Wayne's hand paused, hovering over a photograph he was about to remove. It was the plane crash image, the one he'd stared at countless times before. But now, something caught his eye. In the background of the rescue operation, among the sea of personnel, two figures stood out. Spanish padres, their robes a stark contrast to the military uniforms surrounding them.

His breath caught in his throat. With trembling fingers, he plucked the photo from the board, bringing it closer to his face. The faces of the padres, younger but unmistakable, stared back at him. Was this Trujillo, the cartel boss? Another picture included a person who looked suspiciously like one of the soldiers back on the military base. Wayne's mind reeled. The gold pieces in his pocket suddenly felt heavy, burning against his thigh through the fabric. With his free hand, he fished them out, holding them up next to the photograph. The room around him faded away. Elizabeth's voice became a distant murmur. All he could see were the faces in the photo and the glint of gold in his palm. Pieces of a puzzle he thought he'd solved began to shift and rearrange themselves in his mind.

His eyes widened as the full implications of what he was seeing crashed over him. The military conspiracy, the cartel, the padres - it was all connected, a web of deception far more intricate than he'd ever imagined. Wayne's gaze snapped up from the photo, his eyes wide with shock and a renewed determination. The treasure hunt wasn't over. Behind him, Elizabeth continued to pack, humming softly to herself, completely unaware that their world was about to be turned upside down once again.

THE END

You can watch 'Lost Padre Mine,' the theatrical film version of this novel, on Amazon Prime, Tubi, Movie Central, Xumo, Local Now, Yidio, and other global streaming services.

David Noble

ABOUT THE AUTHOR

David Noble is a native of Tampa, Florida, growing up on adventure movies. By middle school he and a group of willing accomplices started making no-budget action movies, which would transition into a degree in Communications from the University of Tampa. In spite of joining the military, David found time to make several short films, turning to feature films by 2011. After several attempts in the horror, martial arts, and fantasy genres, David wrote, produced, and directed "Lost Padre Mine," an independent feature film available on many video streaming services today. David's film works have been awarded and recognized in over 30 film festivals. While David continues work on future novelizations, you can read his recent novelization of the feature film "Secret Within the Sphere," based on steampunk-themed science fiction. Other movies online to watch include "ZYDECO" and "Knight Squad."

David Noble